1.50

A SMALL
BEQUEST

GREAT LAKES BOOKS

A SMALL
BEQUEST

Edmund G. Love

WAYNE STATE UNIVERSITY PRESS   DETROIT   1987

91   90   89   88   87   5   4   3   2   1

Library of Congress Cataloging-in-Publication Data

Love, Edmund G.
   A small bequest.

   (Great Lakes books)
   I. Title.   II. Series.
PS3562.O84S6   1987   813′.54   87–16202
ISBN 0–8143–1925–4
ISBN 0–8143–1926–2 (pbk.)

To Andy and Janet

A SMALL
BEQUEST

PROLOGUE

My grandfather Love passed away in the fall of 1933. He had been ill for many years and whatever money he had when he was young had long since been used up in his struggle against disease and old age. When his will was read, to our great surprise, he left my brothers and myself a legacy. It was described as "two sections of land in the southwest quadrant of Luce County, Michigan," and the exact land tract numbers were duly included.

No one seemed to know about this land. Even my grandmother Love couldn't remember anything about it. She didn't know when he had acquired it, or why. My grandfather had evidently been very closemouthed about it. Grandmother surmised that he might have bought it in the spring of 1884. At that time he had been foreman of a lumber camp in the upper peninsula and he had been engaged in logging operations in the area around Big Manistique Lake which was, indeed, in Luce County, Michigan.

A preliminary investigation conducted by my father's attorney mystified us. For all intents and purposes, the land appeared to be worthless. It was scrubland, useless for growing purposes because of its sandy soil. It had no timber on it. There were no mineral deposits in the area. It did border on Big Manistique Lake—comprising the whole north shore of that body of water, as a matter of fact. But it was undeveloped and there were no access roads into it. The attorney estimated that it might be worth five cents an acre, or about fifty dollars. He suggested that if we got an offer for it in that amount we'd better take it. Otherwise, it would be better to let it revert to the state. The taxes on it amounted to about ten dollars a year.

That winter of 1933–34 was a Depression winter. Everyone was broke. We were. Neither my brothers nor I were inclined to pay out ten dollars of our good money in taxes for worthless land. Without actually discussing the matter, I think we were agreed that when the tax bill came we would just forget about it. Yet, in the back of our minds there was a puzzling question. Why had Grandfather Love gone along for fifty years keeping up the taxes on this property if it was worthless? Grandfather had been a Scot and in almost all his dealings he had a reputation of being tightfisted. In later years the expenditure of ten dollars for taxes would have been a burden for him. At least once in that winter my father expressed the opinion that there might be more to this than our attorney had been able to find out. He thought someone ought to go up to the upper peninsula and look the situation over before that tax bill came. We were all working that winter and jobs were valuable. None of us were inclined to take the necessary time off to make the trip. The year 1934 drifted into the spring and we more or less forgot about it.

In May 1934, a letter arrived at our house addressed to my father. It was written in pencil, in rather poor handwriting. It was postmarked "Germfask, Michigan." The signature was that of a man named Alec MacKenzie. Mr. MacKenzie identified himself as an old friend of Grandfather's from the logging days. He had just learned of Grandfather's death and had been informed that my brothers and I had been willed "the property on Manistique Lake." He wondered what disposition had been made of it. If it was available, he was prepared to make us a small offer for it.

The words "small offer" were bound to reinforce the low opinion we already had of the property. The figure that kept running through my mind was the fifty-dollar one that had, of course, been planted there by the attorney. When my father finished reading the letter he once more suggested that it might be a good idea if someone went up to the upper peninsula and looked things over. He meant me. The situation had changed since winter and I was now out of work and I was eminently available for such a trip. I didn't want to go. I was hoping to go back to college in the fall and I was looking for another job which I expected to find momentarily. I argued against it. I had no transportation. The family car was on its last legs and I certainly didn't want to hitchhike four hundred miles up there. Furthermore, it would be unprofitable. After the costs of the trip, title transfer fees, and other expenses were deducted from that fifty dollars, we'd end up owing money. I advocated writing to Mr. MacKenzie, finding out what his offer was, and taking it. My father still wasn't satisfied. During the next two months he would bring up the subject at least once a week. I was gradually being conditioned for the trip.

ONE

In the late spring and early summer of 1934 I had two major preoccupations. I was unemployed and my best friend, George French, was acting strangely.

Unemployment brought a long string of worries with it. I had been laid off from a relatively good job in about the middle of the month of May. The foreman in the auto factory where I worked had told me that I need not expect to be called back to work before November. I had one hundred dollars in my pocket at the time I was laid off. There was no such thing as unemployment insurance in 1934. That one hundred dollars had to last me until I got back to work. I was lucky in one respect. I was living at home and had no worries about food and lodging, but that was not of much help to my peace of mind. I felt guilty about sponging off my father who had his own financial problems. Furthermore, unless I did have money coming in, it was foolish to expect to be able to live in the style to which I was accustomed. Quite naturally, from the moment I was laid off, I recognized the fact that I must find a new job. My prospects were bleak. My own factory was not the only one that was shut down. All the factories were closed for the summer.

Although I had a wide acquaintanceship in the city of Flint where I lived, and although I assiduously contacted every person I knew, none of them could help me. Everyone had his own troubles in those years of the Depression and a person could not expect much help. I even checked out the possibilities in the new work relief programs then being opened up by the federal government. That was hopeless because work relief was reserved to married men with families. The only thing of this nature available to a young single man of twenty-two was the Civilian Conservation Corps. That required a one-year period of enlistment, a step that I was unwilling to take. By the end of June, a month after I was laid off from my job, I was reduced to answering the Help Wanted advertisements in the local paper. There were very few of them, and thousands of men were out of work. Everywhere I went to answer one of those ads I found long lines ahead of me. Sometimes there would be two hundred people looking for one job.

My money dwindled steadily. It went down to ninety-five dollars, then ninety, then eighty-five. In attempts to preserve it I took desperate measures. I even gave up riding the streetcars in my job hunt. I was literally walking the streets. I walked them from one end of the town to the other. On some days I walked as much as twelve miles. I was discouraged and frustrated.

George French was something else. We had been close friends since both our families moved to Flint. We lived about a block apart. We went to the same school. We peddled papers together. We belonged to the same Boy Scout troop. We played ball together. One rarely saw one of us without seeing the other. George had a tremendous influence on me. He was better at everything than I was and he was a born leader. As time passed he became the center of an increasingly wide circle. In the Boy Scouts, he became an Eagle Scout and became the chief of the Senior Scouts' Advisory Council. When we went to high school he became a star athlete, captain of the basketball team, and president of our senior class. I looked up to him. I copied his attitudes and tried to emulate him. In those days before college this meant that I set pretty high goals for myself for George was a little like Sir Galahad then, a boy with lofty ideals and high principles. He was good for me.

When it came time to go to college, George and I went different ways. He went to Michigan State and I went to the University of Michigan. The Depression interrupted our studies and by 1931 we were both back home again, wallowing in the depths of those hard times. We continued to be close chums. When we could scrape the money together we played golf or went to the movies. George was a gifted mechanic. His passion was old cars. When we were still in the ninth grade he had gone down to a junk yard and bought an old 1919 Model T Ford coupé for ten dollars. George had to load it on a truck to get it home. He took that old car apart, piece by piece. One evening I went over to his house and found the whole thing laid out on blankets in his back yard. Every nut had been removed from every bolt. Even the screws had been removed from the body. George worked for a year on that car. If he found a worn part that was unserviceable he would buy a replacement for it out of his newspaper money. If a replacement wasn't available he would make one on the machines in the shops at school. When he was done that car purred. It ran better than it ever had when it was new. He drove it for a year while he worked on another piece of junk. In all the time I'd ever known him there was never a day when there was not a car in some stage of rebuilding in his back yard. And in those days after we came back from college, those days when neither of us had much money, I spent a lot of my time in the workshop he had set up in his garage. I wasn't much of a mechanic myself, but I could follow instructions and I could run errands for him.

The Depression was harder on George than it was on

me. My father was slowly going broke, but the Depression killed his father. In 1934, my family was still living in the house we'd always occupied, but George's family had lost their house and were now living in a small, rented, two-bedroom wooden-frame tenement about three blocks away. There were times in those years when I don't think the French family had very much to eat. On the surface George remained imperturbable, but I think his misfortunes were gradually getting to him.

In those years of the early Depression I was a good boy. By "good" I do not mean prissy. I had acquired the habit of smoking cigarettes. I had learned to take an occasional drink. Even in matters of sex, I had undergone my baptism of fire. When I say that I was good I simply mean that after due consideration my family and the family friends had at last arrived at the conclusion that I was not going to do anything that would disgrace the family name. As late as 1933, George still hadn't smoked his first cigarette. He hadn't taken his first drink. As far as I knew he'd had no experiences with girls, but then, I wouldn't have known anyway because that was the kind of thing he wouldn't have talked about. It was against his knightly code of ethics. Then it happened.

In about the middle of the summer of 1933, I introduced George to a rather well-built girl who worked as a waitress in a restaurant near my father's lumberyard. One Sunday morning about three o'clock I was awakened by a tearful phone call from the girl. She wanted me to come to her father's house right away. I did. I found George staggering around the front yard in only his underwear shorts. He was very drunk and he was using just about the most obscene language I ever heard. He wanted the girl to come down on the lawn and do what she was supposed to do. When I tried to reason with him, he informed me that the only reason the girl wouldn't allow him to have his way with her was because he wouldn't tell her he loved her. I managed to get him out of there before the girl's father and mother came home, but in the car on the way back to his house he simply tipped up the bottle he had in his hand and finished it off. Then he passed out.

I had a couple of talks with him about that episode, but I wasn't exactly talking from strength. I didn't know enough about the subject. I do recall that I told him that it would have been better if he had told the girl he loved her. That way the whole thing would have been resolved quite simply.

"But I didn't love her," he said. "That would have been dishonest and I'm not going to be a hypocrite."

He had me there. Just a month after that we went down to Chicago to see the World's Fair. He spent a lot of time visiting the burlesque houses and finally proposed that we all go and spend the night at a whore house. I refused. He and two of our companions went off and stayed out all night and when George came back the next morning he was drunk again. The worst part of it was that all the way home he kept accusing me of being a sissy. I patiently explained to him that the reason I didn't go to the burlesque shows was because I didn't see any sense in them. The jokes weren't funny and the girls weren't pretty. I could see better leg shows in the Keith vaudeville shows at home. The reason I wouldn't go to a whore house was because half the fun I got out of sex came from the chase. I don't think I made any impression on him at all.

Nevertheless, during the winter of 1933–34 we patched up whatever differences we had and went on chumming together. George had a good job that winter and early in the spring he was promoted to foreman of his department. For a young man of twenty-two in those kind of times, this was a major break. It meant that he was on salary and that he was guaranteed year-round employment. It meant, also, that he was definitely *going to go someplace*. His future loomed ahead of him considerably brighter than mine did.

He most certainly deserved the promotion for he was an extremely capable young man.

George blew the whole works. At about the same time I was being laid off he suddenly punched his boss in the nose one day and walked out of the plant. He went home and packed a suitcase and disappeared. I didn't see him for a month. I wasn't with him during those thirty days, of course, and so I have no firsthand knowledge of his trip, but he told me the whole story after he got back. He'd hopped a freight train and had gone all the way to Los Angeles. The day he got there he bought a bottle and got drunk. While in this condition he went into a bar and picked up a girl. She took him to a hotel room, called in a confederate, and together they beat him mercilessly and took all his money. He spent several days in a hospital recovering from the assault and then limped home with his tail between his legs the same way he went—by freight train. George never did make it clear to me why he had done what he had done, but it didn't make sense to me. I gave him a little lecture about reading the wrong books, but what I had to say made no impression on him at all. I was now thoroughly alarmed about him.

In those first days after his return home, I did what I could to buck up George's spirits. I wasn't in very good spirits myself, but I managed to get him to start looking for a job. I co-ordinated our job-hunting efforts. I very generously split the town between us. He could answer all the want ads in the south end of town and I could answer the ones in the north end. I introduced the element of efficiency. At two o'clock each afternoon, one or the other of us would rush to the Flint *Journal* and get the newspaper when it came off the press. Half an hour later we would rendez-vous at some predetermined place to split up the most promising new ads and decide which one would go after which job.

All through this period my father was bringing up the

subject of my grandfather's property. I firmly ignored it.
Each morning I got up in the firm belief that this was the
day that I was going to find that job. I didn't want to be way
off in the upper peninsula when the opportunity came. Still,
something was registering. Ever since the Depression had
started there had been an old saying among the unemployed. "If things really get bad," they would say, "I'll take
off for the north woods. There's plenty of fish and game up
there and a man can live pretty good." Just how many people actually tried this, I don't know, but some of my
acquaintances had, indeed, gone up north during the long
summer layoffs. I don't think very many of them had lived
off the land, but they could build shacks or camp out along
the rivers and lakes and live considerably cheaper than
they could at home in the city. Bit by bit the idea nudged
itself into my mind. I actually owned some property up
north now, and it was supposed to be on a lake. If worst
came to worst I had a last resort. Unfortunately, that's just
what it remained. I was a city boy through and through.
I had never gone hunting. I didn't particularly care for
fishing. The only camping experience I'd ever had dated
back to the time I was in the Boy Scouts and I remembered
it with no particular fondness. I wasn't very handy with
tools. I don't think I would have done anything about it,
if George French hadn't been who he was and what he
was, and if I hadn't been worried enough about him to split
up my job hunting with him.

One late June day, when it was my turn to get the paper
off the press, I made a date to meet George on the corner
of South Saginaw and Seventh Street. By chance this meeting took place directly in front of a used-car lot. It was a
burning hot afternoon and both of us were sweaty and tired
and our feet hurt from pounding the streets.

"You know what I'd like right now?" George asked me.
"I'd like a great big lake. I'd like to dive in it and swim in it
and float in it and drink it."

I agreed that this would be very nice, but then I thrust the paper at him. "George, there's an ad in here that you might get. They want a carhop at a drive-in spot. It's right up there on the corner of Twelfth Street." I pointed. "It's in your territory. If you hurry you might get it."

George nodded and looked at the paper. "If I wasn't so pooped I'd run up there. Maybe I'll run anyway."

He turned around to leave and then he stopped in his tracks. He stood there, frozen, as though he was unable to move. I could see that he was staring at something on the used-car lot and I turned to see what it was. George was looking at the car of his dreams. It was an ancient, 1916 model, Buick touring car. Straps ran down from the top to the tips of the front fenders. Its black body shone from a coat of polish that someone had recently applied. Its high, yellow wheels gave it an aura of genteel stylishness. It was a truly noble vehicle. Even I knew that.

George took it all in from his position on the sidewalk and then he moved slowly toward it. Almost on tiptoe he circled it once, twice, three times, and then the words began to come. It had the first electric-lighting system ever installed on a car of that class, he told me. The upholstering was genuine leather. The gas and spark levers were on the steering wheel. The self-starter was exactly the same as it was when Kettering invented it. There were a hundred features on that car that I would never have noticed, but George ticked them off, one by one. He was in rapture.

While we stood there taking it all in a man came up behind us.

"Are you boys interested in that car?" he asked us.

"Is it for sale?" George asked, without turning around.

"It is," the man said. "Twenty dollars. I'll throw in half-year license plates and eight spare tires." (Things were so bad in Michigan that year that the state was selling license plates on the installment plan.)

"Does it run?" George said, still staring at it.

"Get in and drive it around the block," the man said. "You'll see."

George tenderly opened the door and slid under the wheel, then motioned for me to go around and get in on the other side. After carefully trying all the levers that he could see, George reached out a foot and pushed on the long old starter that stuck out under the dash. There was a grinding, slow at first, and then there was a bang and a cloud of blue smoke as the motor caught and then roared out in full throat. George moved the gear shift lever around and then pulled it back into low. There was a slight shudder and the old car inched ahead. In a small cloud of blue smoke we rolled out of the used-car lot and turned to move down South Saginaw Street. We reached Eighth Street in high gear, turned the corner, and headed west. The motor never skipped a beat. It took us about ten minutes to make the circuit of the block. It had been a splendid voyage. George backed the car into its accustomed place on the lot and said the words I dreaded to hear.

"Lend me twenty bucks. I want to buy this car."

I knew the touch was coming long before it arrived. I'd pushed the panic button in my mind ten minutes before. I had eighty dollars. It had to last me until November. I might not ever get this twenty back if I lent it to George. I knew he was flat broke. And at that particular moment I was more than a little skeptical of him. Only a month before he had more money than I did, but he had thrown it all away. Not only that. His recently demonstrated proclivity for getting drunk and visiting whore houses indicated that he might have a flaw in his character. I think George knew exactly what I was thinking. When I didn't immediately reach into my pocket and come up with the twenty-dollar bill, he tried to make it look good.

"Don't worry about getting the money back," he said. "I'll pay it back somehow. I think I still have twenty dollars coming from the plant. I'll go get it. Just give me the money so I can get this car."

I needed time to think about it. "I haven't got twenty dollars, George. I mean I haven't got it with me. It's home in my dresser drawer."

"Well, let's go home and get it before somebody buys this thing right out from under our nose."

"Not so fast, George. Not so fast. I want to think about this awhile."

"Don't you trust me?"

"Sure I trust you, George, but I've got to get through until I get back to the factory. If I only had some kind of a job it would be different, but I don't have a job and I don't think I'm going to get one."

"You can always live off your old man," he said. "I want this car. I got to have this car."

"Well, I want to think about it. I'll let you know. Right now I have to go and see about that job in the restaurant." I got out of the car and began to walk away.

"Just don't think about it too long," he called after me. His voice sounded so forlorn that it almost broke my heart.

I thought about it. I thought about it all afternoon and into the evening and in the process I finally came up with what I thought was the perfect solution. When I went over to his house, I put my proposition in front of him.

"I'll make a deal with you, George," I told him. "I'll buy the car if you think you can fix it up so that it will get us to the upper peninsula and back. I want to look at some property my grandfather bought up there. Do you think you can get that old wreck up to Manistique Lake and back?"

"How far is it?"

"I don't know. Four hundred miles, I guess."

"I can push it that far. Give me the twenty bucks."

"Not so fast. Now here's the deal. I'll buy the car. We'll drive it up north. We'll camp out on my grandfather's property. I've got sixty bucks left after buying the car. With that and the fish we catch, we ought to be able to live pretty well until fall. We'll come back when the factories open up and our problems will be over. When we get back you can have the car. You won't have to pay me back the twenty bucks."

He stuck out his hand. "It's a deal," he said.

George was so anxious to get that car that I don't think he once stopped to consider the position he had put himself in. I wasn't exactly giving him twenty dollars. I was paying him for services to be rendered. On the surface what I expected of him was transportation, but there was more to it than that. I was making the trip for two reasons, to look over that property and to live a simple existence that would save me money. I wanted company, which George would provide. I also wanted his know-how. Since he had achieved the exalted rank of Eagle Scout, I assumed that those merit badges meant that he could take care of himself —and me—in the great outdoors. I overlooked completely the fact that he was as confirmed a city boy as I was. The only thing in life that he really cared about was tinkering with old cars. Not once in all the years since he was goaded into his last overnight hike by an enthusiastic scoutmaster had he exhibited any interest whatsoever in camping, hunting, fishing, or the outdoors. We were going to be two babes in the woods.

TWO

From the moment we shook hands complete disagreement and disappointment were never far away. It began the next morning at eight o'clock when we showed up at the used-car lot with a twenty-dollar bill in our hand. The salesman dutifully filled out the papers and provided us with the half-year license plate sticker. Then he went into the back room of the little shack on the lot and came forth with eight tires and threw them into the back seat with a gesture that implied good riddance. George and I got into the car and once again there was that slow grinding noise from the starter followed by the big bang and the cloud of blue smoke. George listened to the motor with satisfaction and shook his head.

"Before we start out," he said, "we ought to give this old car a name. I've got an idea."

"What is it?"

"Since this is the granddaddy of all cars, we ought to call it Old Grandad."

"We might get sued by the whiskey people," I said. "Let's try something a little different. How about calling it Old Pappy."

Old Pappy it was and Old Pappy immediately showed us just how crotchety he could be. On that first trial run we had circled a block, almost all of it situated on level ground. Now, in order to get the car to George's house, we had to go four miles. In the middle of that four miles was the Garland Street hill, a three-block stretch at an incline of about thirty degrees. Somewhere in the deep recesses of my childhood memories was a scene that I had forgotten. When I was about three or four years old my father and mother had taken me on a picnic. We had come to a steep hill and my father had made my mother and me get out and walk up the hill while he tried to get the car up. He'd struggled with that operation for half an hour and had finally made it to the top only by getting back a mile and getting a good run at it. Until George and I started up the Garland Street hill I had forgotten completely that one of the big deficiencies of those early cars was in the hill-climbing department. Old Pappy hadn't forgotten. We blithely sailed onto the lower slopes and started up. Old Pappy immediately slowed down. At a point about one third of the way up, Old Pappy began to buck and George quickly shifted into second gear. We progressed a little farther and Old Pappy bucked again. George shifted into low gear. We arrived at a point thirty feet from the top and there Old Pappy gave up. We backed around into a driveway and started the motor and headed back down the hill. Three times we made a run at that hill and three times we stalled a few feet from the top. On the last of those runs I dutifully got out and took the eight spare tires with me to lighten the load. It did no good.

"There's a loss of power here somewhere," George said.

"Maybe there never was any power there in the first place," I said.

"It's got six cylinders, hasn't it? I'll fix it. In the meantime, we'd better find a way home that doesn't involve going up hill."

We found it, but we had to detour two miles out of our

way and come up on George's house from the rear. When we got the car into the back yard George went into the house and got a tablet and a pencil. Then he started walking around and around the car and writing things down. After about an hour he showed me the list he had made. There were about sixty things on it.

"Those are the first things that have to be done," he said. "There may be more when I get it torn down."

"Wait a minute now, George," I said. "This is a lot of things. It will take you six months to do everything you have on this list."

"Well, you want me to drive you up to see your grandfather's property, don't you?"

"Yes, but I want to go this summer, not next year."

"Well, all these things need fixing. I couldn't guarantee this job without doing that much. What I'd really like to do with this is to tear it completely apart and rebuild it from scratch."

"George, our agreement was to drive up to Manistique Lake and camp out on my grandfather's property until it is time to go back to work again. Now, let's be reasonable."

"To hell with the agreement," he said. "I hadn't looked this thing over when I agreed to that."

"Okay," I said. "To hell with the agreement." I went around to the driver's side of the car and climbed up into the front seat and pushed on the starter.

"What are you doing?" George said.

"I'm taking this car home." I pulled out the title the salesman had given me. "I paid for it and the title is in my name. I'll take it back down tomorrow and get my money back."

The motor roared out and the blue smoke spewed forth and I backed down the driveway into the street. It didn't take George long to get down to my house. In fact, he almost got there as soon as I did. He could run almost as fast as Old Pappy could perambulate.

"Now, let's talk this over," he said.

"What do you want to talk over?"

"I want the car. I'll do it your way."

He got out his list and began checking things off. After each item I asked him if this was essential. We agreed on three things that had to be done. The rest could wait until we got back from up north. First, we would overhaul the motor so that Old Pappy would climb hills. Second, we would do something about the tires which, on close inspection, proved to be something less than in perfect condition. Those that we found unsafe would be replaced by spares. Third, we would fix the lights. They didn't seem to work. If we had time we would adjust the brakes and patch up the muffler. In order to save as much time as possible, I would help with the work. We drove the car back up to George's place and into the garage and lifted the hood.

We worked sixteen or seventeen hours a day on Old Pappy for two solid weeks. As we worked, the problems multiplied. The very first thing George did was to pull the valves and regrind them. Two of them were so badly scored that he didn't think they were worth using. He sent me down to the Buick garage to buy two new valves. That was when I got my first shock. The Buick garage didn't have two valves for a 1916 model lying around. Despite the fact that Buicks were made right there in Flint, there wasn't a valve that old in the whole city. This should have told us both something, but it didn't. George quit working on the motor for a day and we visited every parts dealer and rummaged through all the junk yards. In disgust, George put the old valves back in the car, but not before he sarcastically pointed out that if I gave him an extra week he could make a whole new set of valves in a machine shop. When he came to the bearings, he had similar trouble. Still, at the end of two weeks, when he finally put the motor all back together, it ran beautifully. It didn't smoke any more and it didn't pop and bang as it had done when we first got it. To show just how good a job George had done on it, I can testify as to the results of our first trial run. We headed straight for the Garland Street hill and went right to the top without changing gears.

In the meantime, after I had helped George get the motor torn down, he put me to work on other things. I was first put in charge of the tires. I took all eight of the spares up to the nearest gas station and blew them up. They all held air. This little test wasn't enough for George. He inspected them carefully and also looked over the ones that were already on the wheels. It was his considered opinion that they wouldn't last very long and he finally convinced me that it would be best if I went out and bought at least two brand-new tires. There hadn't been any new valves for a 1916 Buick and I now discovered that there weren't any new tires for one, either. No one had made a cord tire since balloon tires had come into general use in about 1923, and no one made a balloon tire that would fit those big yellow wheels. Once more George knocked off work and came to help me look, without success. In some discouragement, he told me to at least take off the tires that were on the wheels and put on the spares. The spares seemed a lot better. Almost immediately I ran into more trouble. I blithely got out the lug wrench to do the changing. No one had changed a tire on that car in fifteen years and the lugs had rusted onto the wheel bolts. I couldn't budge them and neither could George. He sent me up to the neighborhood hardware store for some penetrating oil and I smeared it on liberally and let it set overnight. The next morning the lugs still wouldn't budge so I put on more oil. Every morning for two weeks I tried those lugs. They wouldn't turn. The time for our departure arrived and the lugs were still there. We had a long debate about what to do. We finally decided to start out. Sooner or later that penetrating oil would work and we could change the tires. We were particularly worried about the right front tire. It had a hole in it that looked much like the hole in the sole of a pair of shoes. It was about the size of a dime. It was only going to be a question of time before that tire blew out. All we could do was hope that the penetrating oil would work before it did.

In the meantime, we had another crisis. George turned his attention to the lights. It was a primitive lighting system and it must have worn out years before. For the better part of a day George traced the wiring, locating short circuits and broken wires. At the end he simply shook his head. The lights were unrepairable. The only thing he could do was tear the whole thing down and build a new system from scratch. He estimated it would take two weeks. By then it was the middle of July and I think George was as anxious to get started and get the whole thing over with as I was.

"We can either stay here and fix it, or we can hole up when it gets dark every night," he said.

We decided to go and plan our journey so that we could get off the road before it got dark.

This decision was made somewhere around the sixteenth of July 1934, and we set our departure date for the twenty-first, which was a Sunday. While the repairs on the car were going forward, I had spent some time in getting camping equipment together. I'd managed to borrow two pup tents from neighbors. We had several blankets. A wide variety of miscellaneous camping equipment such as pots and pans, flashlights, lanterns, and digging tools had been stored in the back seat. One unusual item of equipment had turned up. One evening I had gone over to see my grandmother in Flushing to see if she could remember anything more about the property. She told me to go out to the old tack room in the barn where Grandfather's papers had been stored. I might find a map of the Manistique Lake area in there. I didn't find the map, but I did find some round cans lined up along a beam at the back of the room. On the labels was the legend "Monkey Tire Patch." They must have been sitting there for twenty years. I figured that as long as we had an eighteen-year-old car I might just as well take the cans along.

On the two or three days preceding our departure, following George's usual procedure, we took Old Pappy out for trial runs. We discovered that our maximum speed would be about twenty-five miles an hour. That was about all the old car would do. On long grades it had a tendency to slow down to around ten miles an hour, but we didn't find a hill that we couldn't negotiate and we were satisfied. When we got back to George's house after the last trial run, George stood back with his hand on his chin and shook his head dubiously.

"If we don't have too much tire trouble," he said, "we ought to be able to make it up there and back. Just pray that the penetrating oil works before we have a blowout. I sure wish I'd had enough time to work on this thing properly. I could have made a good car out of it."

I patted him on the back. "Just think of how much fun you're going to have working on it this winter," I said. "This ought to be your masterpiece."

After that little conversation, I went up to the grocery store and performed my last chore. I laid in a small supply of groceries, of which the most important item was a full slab of bacon. I was in for one more shock. Before I went to bed that Saturday night I counted my money. Between buying parts for the car and groceries, I'd spent considerably more than I had planned on. Instead of sixty dollars, I had the sum total of forty-three dollars. At that I was better off than George. He didn't have a penny. I was dubious, but by then we'd gone so far that I couldn't back out.

On Sunday morning, July 21, 1934, at quarter of five—just as daylight came—George French backed Old Pappy out of his driveway and we headed for the north woods.

THREE

I was now embarked on an expedition that was to make a city man out of me forevermore. I don't think there has ever been six weeks in a young man's life which had more to do with shaping his future attitudes. In those days before World War II, it was not customary to dub expeditions with intriguing names, but looking back at it from a distance of forty years, I am tempted to describe that innocent little trip by giving it the title OPERATION TOTAL DISASTER. The first indications of what I was in for were not long in coming.

When we left George's house on that gray Sunday morning we headed for U.S. 10, the main highway that led north. The first leg of our trip was the thirty-three-mile stretch to Saginaw. At that time, U.S. 10 was a newly completed four-lane highway. We rolled along over it without mishap, staying well over in the right-hand lane. Our elapsed time was slightly under two hours so that we arrived on the outskirts of Saginaw at around six-thirty. As we rolled along an increasing number of cars came up behind us. Some of them just whizzed by, but not a few of them slowed down to look us over. Now and then we were on the receiving end of wisecracks, but we didn't hear most of them because Old Pappy's muffler didn't muffle anything. We understood, however, that most of the things being said to us were good-natured. We could tell this by the grins on people's faces as they looked us over. Between Flint and Saginaw we stopped twice by the side of the road and I ran forward with the lug wrench to see if the penetrating oil had worked yet. It hadn't. We were still worried about that right front tire which had a hole in it.

That first leg was the only trouble-free leg we were to have. The second leg was twenty-seven miles long. It ran from Saginaw up along the inner shore of Saginaw Bay to the junction town of Standish. The road was paved and fairly level. The car ran well. Unfortunately, we were traveling on a Sunday morning in July, at the very height of Michigan's tourist season. And that twenty-seven-mile stretch of road was a bottleneck. All traffic from the south was funneled into it at Saginaw. All traffic from the north was funneled into it at Standish. Tourists, fishermen out for a day's sport in the woods, families bent on an outing along the Saginaw Bay and Lake Huron beaches, and just plain Sunday drivers were all making early starts that morning. We rolled from Saginaw out on that narrow road at our usual twenty-five miles an hour, slowing down to fifteen on the grades. Traffic flowed at us steadily from the north. Traffic behind us began to pile up. It began to pile up in spectacular fashion. Now and then, when there was a break in the oncoming traffic, a car would duck out from behind us and whirl past. Quite early, I noticed, we weren't getting any more good-natured grins. Later I began to catch the sound of swear words wafted back to us on the wind as the cars whizzed by. Twelve miles north of Saginaw we pulled over to the side so that I could test the lugs on the front tire. Sixty cars or more picked up speed and moved past us. Every single one of those sixty drivers gave us a dirty look. Some of them called us names. George was considerate.

"Maybe we'd better pull over oftener," he said.

We did. We went six miles and pulled off to the side again. This time we had thirty-seven cars backed up behind us. About five miles south of Standish, when we pulled off the fourth time, George looked at me.

"How many cars do you think are back there now?"

"From the sound of the horns, I'd say about twenty-eight," I said.

"More than that," he said. "I'll bet you a nickel there are thirty-five."

"But you haven't got a nickel."

"I soon will have."

There were thirty-six and George had a nickel in his pocket. We had established a pattern. We were about to establish another.

Standish was a main highway junction point in Michigan. Northbound travelers had two choices of routes open to them. They could go off to the left and up through the center of the state on U.S. 27, eventually coming to Mackinaw City. Or they could go off to the right on U.S. 23 and follow the shore line of Lake Huron through the cities of Alpena and Cheboygan. Peculiarly enough, in all our discussions, George and I had not discussed which of the two routes we would take. I think I assumed that we would go up through the center of the state because it was seventy miles shorter. Not only that, but we had a mutual friend whose family owned a cottage near Grayling. Grayling was about five hours from Standish at the speed Old Pappy was making. We would arrive there well before dark and probably get taken in for the night. I was reinforced in this assumption by the fact that George had visited in Grayling twice in the last two years and had spoken fondly of the place.

When we rolled into the outskirts of Standish, I told George to drive over to the big state park. It was my idea to find a fireplace, get out the bacon, and cook us a meal. George drove to the state park, all right, and we threaded our way slowly up and down the little lanes. The place was jammed with people. Every single fireplace was taken.

"The hell with this," George said, after we'd made our second circuit of the place. "Let's go find a restaurant and buy ourselves something to eat."

"That's foolish, George. We've only got forty-three dollars. I don't see any sense of spending any of it when we've got food right here in the car. Just park for a while. Somebody's bound to be leaving here before long."

"Don't be so damned tight," he said. "We've got a hundred and fifteen miles to go. That's a good six hours in this old car and you've got to allow a couple of hours extra for trouble. It's almost nine o'clock and if we're going to get to Alpena by dark, we can't monkey around here waiting for one of those fireplaces to get vacant."

"Alpena? I thought we were going up through Grayling. Why do you want to go by way of Alpena?"

"Because I want to go by way of Alpena, that's why. Do I have to have a reason?"

"Well, sure. It's a lot shorter the other way."

He sat there, glaring at the windshield. I could see him struggling desperately to think up a reason. "Well, there's the traffic," he said finally. "Yeah, that's it. There's a lot more traffic that way."

"The traffic shouldn't slow us down any. We aren't going to pass anybody."

He thought again. "Well, there are a lot more hills on that road. There's one big long one up there at West Branch. We might not be able to make it to the top."

"Oh, come on, George. We've hit a couple of hills already and we haven't had to shift out of high yet. This thing will climb hills all right now."

He thought again. "I know, but just think how slow we are. With all those hills and all these cars on the road, we'd have traffic backed up all the way to Saginaw. I tell you, we have to go by way of Alpena. We've got to."

I was exasperated, but I had to admit he was right. "All right," I said. "We'll go by way of Alpena. Have it your way."

He put the car in gear and we lumbered out onto the highway. At the junction we stopped at a gas station and bought gas. That came to a dollar and a quarter. Just as we were getting ready to climb back in the car, George pointed at a restaurant across the road. "How about something to eat? I'm hungry. A hamburger isn't going to break you."

"All right, George," I said. "Get your damned hamburger. I'll have one, too." I knew I was doing something very wrong when I said that, but I was tired of arguing. Basically, the big mistake I made in giving in to him was in setting a precedent. I should have made it very clear to him that we weren't going to spend money for *anything* except absolute essentials, but I hadn't. As though to confirm my sense of misgiving, the hamburger turned out to be two hamburgers and a pint of milk and I almost crawled under the table when George ordered a piece of apple pie à la mode to top it off. The whole bill came to seventy-five cents. I couldn't help thinking, as we pulled back onto the road, that we were now down to forty-one dollars. We'd been gone from home just five hours and 5 per cent of our money was gone already. At that rate we would run out of money by the end of the first week.

The long leg up to Alpena was a grind. We plugged along at our usual twenty-five miles an hour, stopping every half hour or so to let traffic go by and to check those lugs on the right front wheel. We passed Tawas at two-thirty. On account of two long hills we were a full hour behind schedule getting into Oscoda. At four o'clock I looked at my watch.

"We're still thirty-five miles from Alpena," I said. "I don't think we're going to make it by dark. Maybe you'd better start looking for a camping place along here."

"We'll make it, all right," George said. "We've got to make

39

it. There's a state park there. If we try to camp at any of these places along here, they'll charge us for it."

"All right, but let's cut out all these stops we're making."

"What about the people behind us?"

"To hell with the people behind us. Just keep going."

"What about those wheel lugs?"

"Let's face it, George, they aren't ever going to loosen up."

We plodded ahead. Five o'clock came, then six, then seven. We skirted Thunder Bay and the sun went down. It was just getting dark when we came to the city limits. George drove about three blocks down a shaded city street in the twilight and abruptly turned left. After a block he turned right, then did another right. In a moment we were back on the main street again. He went another block and made another left turn.

"What are you doing?" I asked him.

"I'm looking for something," he said.

"Well, look for the state park. It will be pitch dark in another ten minutes. If we get caught driving around here without any lights, I hate to think what would happen to us."

"Ah," he said, "there it is." He pulled in to the curb in front of a big square house and jumped out and started to walk up to the front door.

"Where are you going?" I said.

"I'll be right back. Keep your shirt on."

He was gone ten minutes. When he came back it was so dark that I couldn't see a thing. He came to my side of the car.

"Look," he said. "I've got to have two dollars."

"What do you have to have two dollars for?"

"I've got a date. I want to take her to a movie and get her something to eat afterwards."

I looked at him and then I exploded. "Why you lousy

dope!" I yelled. "Is that why you came by way of Alpena, so you could see some dizzy dame?"

"Keep your voice down," he said. "She isn't any dizzy dame. She's a real dish. I knew her when I was over to State. She was a coed over there."

"I don't care who she is," I said. "You're not getting any two bucks out of me just so you can have a date with some girl. You seem to think I'm running this trip just for you."

He looked at me as though I'd just hit him between the eyes with a club. "What kind of a guy are you?" he said. "You're getting all worked up over nothing."

"Nothing? Look, George, we've got forty-one bucks. It's got to last us until October, at least. That's three months. You've brought us seventy miles out of our way just so you could see some girl and now you want to spend two bucks of that money, which we can't afford. On top of all that, it's dark and here we are, God knows where. If we try to drive this thing, even from here to the state park, we could get a ticket from the police for driving without lights. We can't even leave it parked here without lights. What kind of a way is that to act?"

In his whole life George had never been mad at me. Now he seemed to pull himself together and he pointed his finger at me. "Now you listen to me," he said. "You talked me into coming along on this trip. I've worked for two weeks and a half getting this car ready so it would run this far. I'm not your flunky and it isn't my fault that you've got all the money. Now, you either give me the two bucks or we'll call it quits right now. I'll hitchhike back home in the morning and you can stick the car and everything in it up your ass." He seemed to relax. "Why don't you think of somebody else besides yourself? I thought of you."

"How? I don't see any evidence of it."

"I got you a date, that's how. With a real good-looking girl too. With Agnes's cousin."

I groaned. "You what?"

"I got you a date so you wouldn't have to sit out here all alone."

"George, that's two dollars more. We're down to thirty-seven dollars. Goddamn it, what's the matter with your head?"

I heard a screen door slam and a sweet feminine voice called out from the darkness.

"George? Are you there?"

He looked at me and put his hand up to his lips. "This is no time to argue. We'll discuss this later. Give me the two dollars."

"You're goddamned right we'll discuss this later," I said in a low voice. I could see a figure in a white dress coming down the sidewalk toward us.

I didn't discuss it later. Agnes turned out to be an extremely attractive girl with a come-on look about her. George introduced me to her.

"Not bad. Not bad," she said. "Wait until you see the girl I have for you. She's a darling." She looked at the old car. "George, you can't leave this parked here in the street. Put it in the driveway." She beckoned to me. "You come on in the house and meet Sue."

There wasn't much I could do. Not really. Of course, if Agnes had been homely, or if my date had turned out wrong, I might have sulked or raised hell, but it just wasn't meant to be. Sue was a tall blonde, just my type and she presented interesting possibilities. That wasn't all that happened when I got in the house. Agnes's mother was waiting for me, busily wiping her hands on her apron. After I'd been introduced, and after George had come in from parking the car, she flapped the apron at us to shoo us out of the house.

"Now you all run along. If you're going to make the last movie, you'll have to hurry. When you come back, I'll have something to eat for you." She cocked her head at me. "I hope you like Polish sausage."

I did like Polish sausage. In fact, I liked everything about

Alpena. We walked along the dark streets to the movie and we walked back again. Sue held my hand and made everything all right. At some time before we got to the movie, I managed to slip George the two dollars he wanted. When we got back to the house after the show, Agnes's mother ushered us out into the kitchen and made us sit down to one of the most wonderful meals imaginable. I ate until I thought it was going to come out my ears. We sat there until one o'clock in the morning and then Agnes's mother shooed George and me upstairs to bed. We slept in the same room with Agnes's brothers so we had to be quiet. When we got up in the morning we went downstairs to find a breakfast table heaped with food. Agnes and her mother and her brothers and Sue sat around the breakfast table until nine o'clock, laughing and talking. At that point we all trooped out and looked at Old Pappy. For the next two hours, we took each person for a swing around Alpena in turn. Finally, at noon, the whole family stood on the lawn and waved good-by to us as we roared away. Under the circumstances, I just didn't feel like continuing my argument with George. I was a little ashamed. I was even ashamed to ask him for the dollar back that he hadn't used. This in spite of the fact that we were down to thirty-six dollars after we bought gas that morning. We just headed north toward Mackinaw City as though nothing had happened.

FOUR

We were never free from trouble for very long. George had done all the driving on the first day. I was to handle that chore on the second day. We had approximately eighty miles to go. We had left Alpena at noon so that we had seven hours before darkness would force us off the road. We anticipated no trouble in reaching our destination, but things could happen.

We were one hour, or about seventeen miles, out of Alpena when I saw the first drops of rain on the windshield. Within five minutes the rain was coming down in torrents. I reached for the windshield wiper. There wasn't any windshield wiper. There wasn't even a hand-operated one. George and I had inspected that car at least a half-dozen times and I don't think either one of us had noticed that there wasn't a windshield wiper. I stopped the car.

"What do we do?" I said.

"We can't just sit here," he said. "Why don't you just drive on? I don't think this will last long. We'll come out the other end of the storm before very long."

"I know, but how do I see where I'm going?"

45

"Just lean your head out around the edge of the windshield," he said.

I put the car in gear and pulled down the gas lever and stuck my head around the corner of the windshield. When one gets north of Alpena, he is in the northern latitudes and there is no such thing as a warm, summer rain. This one was cold and it was driving straight in from the northeast, off Lake Huron. I got the full force of it, right in the face. Within minutes the water was dripping off my eyebrows and the whole upper part of my body was soaked to the skin. George was no better off. The rain was driving in from his side of the car. He edged across the seat toward me until he was sitting right up against me. It didn't do him any good. He couldn't get away from it. Very soon he was as wet as I was. At some time in those first few minutes he turned around and looked into the back seat. Pools of water were forming in the folds of our equipment.

"Damn it," George said. "Everything we have is going to be soaked. Did people drive around in this kind of weather in the old days?"

I searched through my memory. "They had side curtains," I said. "When I was small and it started to rain my father would rush around and put up the side curtains. Didn't your father ever have one of these old cars?"

"We had a horse and buggy. Where did your father keep his side curtains?"

"Under the seat, of course."

"Pull over," George said. "We'll look."

I stopped the car and we got out in the rain. We looked under the front seat. There was nothing there. We began taking all of our things out of the back seat. There was nothing there, either, but by the time we'd finished standing there in that driving rain unloading and loading things back in, we were wet to the bone. I was so cold my teeth were chattering.

46

"I think we've been gypped," George said. "There must have been some side curtains for this car."

"Just remember that," I said. "The next time you buy a 1916 car, look for the side curtains."

We got back in the car and I drove on, still hanging around the front of the windshield, trying to see through the driving rain. Ten minutes after we resumed our journey there was a slight jolt. We had come to the end of the pavement. Ahead of us stretched a gravel road. It was a good gravel road. The trouble with it was that there was gravel on it.

"Did you look at that right front tire back there?" George said to me.

"No. Why?"

"I wonder how big that hole is now. Get out and look at it."

"Nuts to you," I said. "If you think I'm going to get out in this rain again you are wrong."

"Why not?" He looked me up and down. "You're wet already. It won't hurt you to get any wetter."

"I'm no wetter than you are. What do you want to know how big that hole is for?"

"Because I was looking at those gravel stones. I have a hunch that they may just about fit in it. I'd say we ought to have a blowout within the next five minutes."

"You're a cheerful bastard," I said. "What do you want me to do, dodge them?"

"No, but just hang on tight to that steering wheel. When the tire goes, you will be heading straight for the ditch. What I want to know is, what are we going to do about it when it does go?"

"I don't want to think about it. I'd appreciate it if you'd keep your damned mouth shut."

I drove on. The rain came down. It didn't let up and it didn't get any warmer. The gravel stones seemed to be getting bigger and bigger. Under the force of the heavy storm the road got rougher and rougher, like a washboard. The wheel in my hands jiggled as we hit each bump. The water was pouring off my face and I had to bring up my hand every few minutes to wipe my eyes. George was right up against me, all curled up in a ball, his head pulled down inside his jacket. Two o'clock came, then three, then four. There was no change. I didn't know how far we had come or how far we had to go. There were no road signs. Even if there had been, I wouldn't have been able to see them. At a little after five there was another small jolt and the car rode easier. We'd regained the pavement again. Almost immediately we found ourselves in a town. It was Cheboygan. We'd been out more than five hours and we had come sixty miles. We still had twenty to go, but under those heavy, low storm clouds, it seemed to be getting dark already. In Cheboygan, all the lights were on. I gritted my teeth and plunged ahead.

Those last two hours were hell. Now and then cars would pass us coming the other way. They all had their lights on. Cars whizzed by us going our way, too. They also had their lights on. At a little before seven o'clock I could hardly see the road, but some lights loomed in the distance. Doggedly I pushed ahead and saw the sign that marked the limits of Mackinaw City. Beneath it were the arrows directing us to the state park. The pitch blackness descended upon us, but I kept going and finally saw the palisade gate that marked the entrance to the camping area. With a sigh of relief I turned in.

In the summertime, Mackinaw City is the focus of the whole Michigan tourist trade. Hundreds of people camp there, some of them for two or three days at a time. They take trips to Mackinac Island. They wait for the ferry to the upper peninsula. They go on excursions to the inland lakes and to Traverse Bay. Yet, when I turned into the state park that night I had every right to expect that the campers would have run for cover. It had been raining since one o'clock in the afternoon. The wind was blowing a gale. It was so cold you could see your breath. I couldn't believe my eyes. Everywhere I looked there were tents and cars. The place seemed clogged. I drove up one lane and down another. Every square inch was taken. After two circuits of the park, I stopped at the gate and went into the park ranger's office.

"We're pretty full up," he said. "Why don't you try Cheboygan?"

"Because my lights are out with all this rain."

He shrugged and opened the door and pointed out into the night. "Go down that lane right there to the very end. When the road turns, you just go straight on ahead for about twenty feet. You should find a place. Don't go any farther than twenty feet, though."

It was a good thing he said that. I followed his directions exactly and I found myself in a vacant space big enough for the car and the tent. I also found myself on a spit of land that jutted out into some wildly turbulent water. Another ten feet and Old Pappy would have ended up in the Straits of Mackinac. I shook George awake and we piled out. Quickly, and with surprising efficiency, we dragged a pup tent out of the back of the car and began the task of pitching it. When it was up, and while I pulled out the blankets, George took a spade and dug a trench all around the tent in approved Boy Scout fashion. The blankets were soaked through. Before I spread them out, I had to wring them out. Everything in the back of that car was sodden. I pulled some of it out and tried to fit it into the shelter of the tent, but I could hardly make a dent in the pile of things we'd brought with us.

"I'm hungry," George said. "Let's go and eat."

"Let's go where and eat?"

"Into Mackinaw City. There must be some restaurants in there."

"George," I said, "we've eaten in our last restaurant. I already told you that. Go up to the park ranger's and get an armful of wood."

He was gone for twenty minutes, but when he came back he had a big armload of wood. There was one trouble with it. It was all wet. When I pulled out my matches they were wet, too.

"That settles it," George said. "We go into Mackinaw City and eat."

"The trouble with you, George, is that you give up too easy." I pointed along one of the lanes. Somebody had a big fire going in one of the fireplaces. "Bring the wood along. We're going to borrow a fire."

There was a big pyramidal tent beside the fire, but no one seemed to be around. I noticed that the car that should have been there was gone. I didn't waste any time in niceties. I just put a half dozen sticks of our wet wood on the fire and went back to our car and got out a frying pan and the slab of bacon and a loaf of bread. I stood there, huddled over in the rain, and put some bacon in the frying pan. That bacon never did sizzle. Long before it got to the sizzling stage, the pelting rain had half filled the frying pain with water. I grabbed the frying pan handle and dumped out the water and put the bacon back on the fire. Within two or three minutes the pan was filling up again.

"To hell with it," I said. "We'll boil it."

"Whoever heard of boiled bacon?" George said. "You can't boil bacon."

"Well, I'm boiling it," I said. "Get out the bread, George. We'll eat boiled bacon sandwiches."

He picked up the loaf of bread and tore open the paper. "God," he said, "this is soaked through. It's like mush. We can't eat this."

"Put a few slices of it on the grill there, over the fire. That will dry it out. We'll have toasted sandwiches."

I didn't know how long it took to boil bacon. I just let it simmer for ten minutes and then dumped the water out of the pan and turned the slices over. When the pan was filled with water and had boiled for another ten minutes, I lifted it out.

"That don't look done to me," George said.

"It's as done as it's going to get. Hand me a couple of slices of that bread."

I put half the bacon on it and handed it to him, then started to make my own sandwich.

"God, this is awful," George said, making a face.

I took a bite of my own sandwich. I had to agree with him, but I wasn't going to admit it. I took a second big bite and made myself chew it. George sat there on his haunches and stared at his sandwich. Suddenly he stood up and stalked over to the fire and threw the sandwich down on the grill.

"I don't know about you," he said, "but I've had all I'm going to take of this. I'm going into town and get something to eat."

"That's all right with me. What are you going to use for money?"

He fished in his pocket and brought out a soggy one-dollar bill and held it up for me to see.

"But you can't do that," I sputtered. "That's my money."

"It's mine, now. You lent it to me. You coming?"

"Never," I said. "I'll drown first."

I almost did too. I watched him walk away into the night and then squatted there, making myself eat that bacon sandwich. When it was finished, I picked up all the things, including the soggy loaf of bread, and carried them back and put them in the car. Then I got down on my hands and knees and crawled into the tent and lay down. It was like stretching out in a tub of ice cold water. Behind me I could hear the waves of the Straits of Mackinac as they broke over the rocks. With each wave a thin sheet of water would spread out over the spit of land and creep into the tent from the rear. Overhead the rain pelted down. The little trenches that George had dug had long since filled with water and rivers now coursed through and under the blankets. One of them ran right under my buttocks. I lay there, debating whether to get up and dig those trenches deeper.

"The hell with it," I said. "I'll drown first." I rolled over and went to sleep. I have only spent one other night like that in my whole life. That was on Okinawa, eleven years later. I slept well that night, too. I guess the night in Mackinaw City conditioned me for it.

I have no idea what time George came back to the tent. I think it was nearly dawn. A long time later I found out that he stayed in the restaurant until it closed and then spent another two or three hours huddled under the canopy of a gas station. It made no difference. He eventually crawled in beside me and when it came time to get up he was as wet as I was.

It was now Tuesday morning. We'd been gone from home just forty-eight hours.

FIVE

The rain was still pouring down. It hadn't let up a bit since those first drops appeared on the windshield. If I had been older I might have recognized that someone was trying to tell me something. But I wasn't older. I was just stubborn.

When we climbed out of our tent into the cold gray light and looked around, we found that most of the people were breaking camp. They were busy at work packing things away into their nice warm, closed cars. There wasn't a fire in any of the nearby fireplaces.

"Have you had enough, yet, or are you still going to try to boil bacon?" George asked me.

I was hungry. I was miserable. "Lead the way," I said. "It will be worth it just to get in out of this wet."

We sloshed through the mud and downpour for half an hour and slunk into a restaurant like two drowned rats to take seats on stools at the back end of the counter near the stoves. The steam rose off us in clouds as we sat there devouring sausage and pancakes. The waiter brought the check and I paid the dollar without blinking an eye. I didn't even lament the fact that we were now down to less than

53

thirty-five dollars. Buttoning our mackinaws tight about our necks and turning up the collars, we tramped back to the park. Still working in a heavy downpour, we struck the tent and folded it up as best we could and put it in the back with all the other wet things. We did try to wring out the blankets, but it didn't do much good.

When everything was loaded in the back, George crawled up into the driver's seat and turned on the ignition, pushed on the starter. It ground slowly at first, then faster. I kept waiting for the usual bang and the puff of blue smoke, but nothing happened.

"I guess we'd better quit this," George said, finally, "or we'll run down the battery."

"What's the matter with it?" I asked.

"I don't know, but I imagine everything is wet." He got out and lifted up the hood. Water was dripping from every wire and little pools were standing at various places. "I wonder if there is a dry cloth in the back there."

"I'll bet there isn't a dry cloth within a hundred miles of here," I said.

"Well, we'll never get this started unless we find one. What have you got in that suitcase you stuck away in the bottom of the pile there?"

"Some clean clothes. What do you think?"

"Well, they ought to be fairly dry. Get me out an undershirt. That ought to do the trick. Maybe you'd better get out two of them. This is pretty wet."

"What's the matter with using one of your undershirts?" I asked him.

"It's your car, isn't it? If you want it to run, get out the undershirts."

He had me. I began digging through the pile in the back seat and got out the suitcase and opened it to lift out the undershirts. While I was doing it, he rigged up one of the pup tents over the hood so that no new water would get on the motor. Then he went to work. He wiped off every wire.

He took out every spark plug and cleaned it. At the end he dried off the distributor cap. When he was done, he held up crossed fingers and tossed me the greasy, oily undershirts.

"You'd better put them back in the suitcase where they won't get wet," he said. "We may need them again."

"The hell with that noise. They'd get everything else all oily."

He shrugged and swung up into the front seat and pressed on the starter. There was a long grinding and then a chug. Then there was more grinding and two chugs. The last time, just as it seemed to me as though the grinding was slowing down we got our bang and the cloud of blue smoke. George worked the spark and gas levers on the steering wheel in frantic motions and the noise settled down to a steady series of pops and bangs. It sounded terrible, but it was running.

"Give it time to settle down," George said. "It will dry itself out in a minute. I think it's going to live."

He let the motor run steadily at a good speed while we put the tent back in the car. It stopped popping and banging, but it still didn't sound right to me. I told George so.

"It's only running on four cylinders," he said. "It will probably have to run quite a while before those other two plugs start firing. That's those two scored valves in there. They're sticking. Until they get thawed out, they'll keep on sticking."

He got in and put the car in reverse to back out into the park roadway. The minute he let the clutch out the motor slowed right down and began to pop and bang. I thought it was going to die, but George pushed the clutch in and worked the levers and got it going again.

"There's hardly enough power to budge this thing," he said. "You'll have to push."

I pushed and George let the clutch out again. The motor began to pop and bang and slow down, but the car slowly moved backward. When we finally got it out on the roadway, George signaled for me to push it the other way. I ran around to the back and pushed. The car moved forward and rolled steadily along the road. I ran ahead and jumped on the running board and let myself into the seat.

With the motor popping and banging in horrendous fashion, and with the car bucking uncertainly along in low gear we reached the gateway of the park and emerged into the streets of Mackinaw City. Twice we came to stop streets and each time when George tried to get it started again I thought it was going to die. Each time I had to get out and push to give it momentum. We finally made the turn into the main street and headed for the ferry, but even then our transit of the town was uncertain. We banged and bucked along with people coming to the windows to see what all the noise was.

There was a very good reason why most people in Mackinaw City broke camp at the crack of dawn. The state of Michigan ran car ferries across the Straits of Mackinac to St. Ignace in the upper peninsula. Those car ferries were notorious. They were modern steamers in every sense, and they had efficient crews, but there just weren't enough of them. They left Mackinaw City at hour and a half intervals. There were long waits. At the opening of the deer hunting season, when the hunters streamed north, the waits were sometimes twenty-four hours. One November a man I knew got at the end of the ferry line in Cheboygan, twenty miles away, and it took him thirty-six hours just to reach the ferry. Things were almost as bad during holiday weekends in the summer and on almost any Sunday during the tourist season one could count on at least a twelve-hour delay. This was a Tuesday, a miserable, rainy Tuesday, and neither George nor I expected any such wait as that, but it was the tourist season and as we rattled and banged along the highway, passing the long line of cars, we began to get apprehensive. We reached the city limits and drove two miles farther on. There we reached the end of the line. George turned the car around and we came to rest behind the last car. Other cars came along the road and turned around and fell in behind us. We had been sitting there in the same place for fifteen minutes when George stuck his hand out.

"What do you know?" he said. "It's stopped raining."

It had, indeed. All along the line of cars ahead of us we could see doors opening. People got out and stretched and stood looking up at the sky. The man in the car ahead of us lit a cigarette and then came back to stand and look at our old car.

"That's some car you've got there, boys," he said. "But you might just as well shut off the motor. You've got a long wait ahead of you."

"If we shut it off, we might never get it started again," George said. "Just how long do you figure it will be before we catch the ferry?"

He looked at his watch. "Well, they've started loading the six-thirty by this time. We ought to be moving ahead in a few minutes. Let's see, now." He ticked off some figures on the fingers of his left hand. "If we're lucky we might make the eleven o'clock, but twelve-thirty is more like it."

He started to walk around the car, but as he did so his car door opened and his wife pointed ahead. The line was beginning to move. He scrambled back to his own driver's seat and in a moment began to inch forward. We jerked along behind him. Fortunately, by this time, our motor seemed to have regained a little of its power. It backfired and made strange hissing noises, but I didn't have to get out and push to give it momentum. We'd move five or ten feet, stop for a moment, and move forward again. I would have to say that we had gone a little over a mile when we heard the ferry whistle in the distance and then the line stopped moving altogether. Nothing much changed for quite a long time. Ahead of us, I noticed, several of the car owners gathered around a big rock. When I went over to see what they were doing, I discovered they had started a card game.

Several of the women had gathered in another group, but I have no idea what they were talking about. In our car, George had stretched out on the front seat and had gone sound asleep. The motor was still running.

It was probably a little before eight when a stream of cars began to come down the highway toward us. Someone in the card game looked up.

"Well, gentlemen," he said, "the ferry's in. I think I'll get a haircut the next time we stop. We ought to be back in town by then."

I went back to the car and shook George and he sat up and grasped the steering wheel. He pulled down the gas lever and the motor roared out as a big cloud of blue smoke spewed forth from the back. George beamed.

"Hey!" he said. "What do you know? We've picked up another cylinder."

After a few more minutes the line began to inch forward again. We kept moving. Ahead of us the sign for the city limits of Mackinaw City loomed up. We passed it by about thirty feet and then stopped for good. Just ahead of us, and off the road to our right, someone had stuck up a crudely painted sign. It said that if you reached that point you could get on the next ferry.

"Looks like we're going to do better than that fellow thought. If that sign's right, we'll make the eleven o'clock ferry easy."

"That's still three hours, George. You know, if we keep this motor running all that time, we're going to run out of gas."

"I don't dare shut it off. We might never get it started again."

I took a yardstick and went around to the back and stuck it in the tank. There were about three inches of liquid showing. George shook his head when he saw it.

"I don't know," he said. "It's going to be pretty close."

"What do we do, George? We can't drive this thing into

a gas station. If we get out of line, nobody's going to let us back in. We'll have to go all the way back and start over again."

"One of us could go and get a five-gallon can and bring it back here."

"If we can find a five-gallon can."

"Oh, somebody's bound to have a five-gallon can along here. They'll lend it to us." He climbed down from the seat. "I'll go, I need to stretch my legs anyway." He held out his hand. "Give me a dollar."

"You don't need a whole dollar," I said. "They are selling gas for seven gallons for a dollar here. You can't carry seven gallons in a five-gallon can anyway."

"Oh, for Christ's sake," he said. "Give me seventy-five cents then. Don't be such a tightwad."

"I know you by this time. You'll probably get another hamburger."

"I won't get any hamburgers. Give me the money."

I fished the money out of my pocket and peeled off a dollar bill. I watched him walk off down the street and then I climbed back up in the car to keep the motor running. It was well over an hour before I saw George again. The other people were streaming back to their cars and the oncoming traffic was already coming off the nine-thirty ferry when he came struggling up the road with his can of gasoline. I took the cap off the tank and he poured the fluid in.

"I got this at a station a couple of blocks up the street," he said. "We go right by it on the way to the ferry. I'll drop it off when we go past."

"I was beginning to worry about you," I said. "Where have you been for more than an hour?"

"Well, there was quite a line. I had to wait."

"That guy must make a lot of money, furnishing gas for people who use it up waiting for the ferry."

"Oh, I wasn't talking about gas. I was talking about the

barbershop. It seems that everybody goes and gets a haircut while they are waiting for the ferry."

"You mean you got a haircut?" My mouth dropped open.

"Sure," he said, flipping off the white sailor cap he was wearing. His hair was cropped very short, almost down to bristles. "And don't go crabbing about the money. It only costs two bits and I had almost that much left from supper last night." He reached over and grabbed my hat off. "You could use a haircut, yourself, if you ask me. You might not be able to get one up there."

"They have barbers in the upper peninsula."

"I know, but you can't count on it and they might be more expensive. The next time this line stops, you'd better get one."

I felt my hair. It *was* pretty long. In all the work getting ready for the trip, I'd forgotten all about haircuts.

"All right," I said. "I'll get one."

We climbed in the car and the line began moving forward. When we passed the gas station I dropped the can off. When we came to the barbershop, George pointed it out to me.

"You might just as well drop off and go over there right now," he said. "When this line stops moving, it will fill up quick."

I nodded and jumped to the ground and headed across the street. There was one man in the chair and I was the only other person in the shop. I sat down and waited for about five minutes and then I heard the horns blowing outside. The next thing I knew, George stuck his head in the door and shouted at me.

"Hurry up!" he said. "Come on!"

I didn't ask any questions. I ran out of the shop as fast as I could go. We were about a hundred yards from the ferry dock and we must have covered it in about ten seconds. Old Pappy was sitting about twenty feet away from the toll gate, the motor still running. George jumped in the driver's seat and put the car in gear and pointed at the gate where a man was standing with his hands on his hips.

"Pay the man," George shouted.

I fumbled in my pocket and drew out my roll of bills. "How much?" I said.

"I ought not let you on at all, holding up the line like that," the man said. "Six dollars."

I peeled off a five and a one and shoved them at him and ran after George who was halfway across the dock, sputtering and banging away. One of the ferry crewmen was frantically waving him ahead. The car came to the ramp and the crewman directed George to drive past it and back down onto the ramp. I jumped on the running board and climbed in the front seat just as we eased down onto the boat. The minute we were aboard the ramp pulled up and settled into place. It was right up against the front of our car. From somewhere up above I heard the ferry whistle. I looked at George.

"What happened?" I said.

"The line stopped moving and the gate went down. I was the third one from the gate. After a few minutes, the toll collector came down the line and he told me there would be room for three more cars, to be ready to go. So I lit out after you."

"Well, we made it anyway." I looked around. We were absolutely the last car on the boat. They couldn't have squeezed a kiddie car on there. Old Pappy was sitting at an angle, the nose of the radiator about ten feet higher than the back. A crewman was busy stretching chains across the raised ramp to hold it in place and he had to crawl across our hood to do it. He stopped and turned and looked at us.

"Turn off the motor, boys," he said. "It's against the law to let your motor run on this boat."

George started to protest, then shrugged, and turned it off.

"Do you suppose we'll ever get it started again?" I asked him.

"Oh, sure," he said. "We were hitting on all six cylinders there at the toll gate. I think the old can is all right now."

The ferry ride to St. Ignace was an hour and a half long. It was ordinarily a very pleasant trip and most people got out and walked around the decks and enjoyed it. But this particular morning the sky was still dark and ugly and a stiff wind was blowing. The water was rough and it was cold. When we got up to the ship's cabin, we found all the people jammed in. There wasn't a seat to be found. We went out on deck and stood, but it was so cold we were both shivering. George looked down at his blue coat.

"Now I know why they call these things mackinaws," he said. "A guy wouldn't be able to live without one up here, even in the summertime."

"Cheer up, George. You'll dry out and the weather will get warmer. Of course, we may starve to death before we get done with it at the rate we're spending money. After paying the fare on this boat, we've only got twenty-six bucks left."

"That's plenty of money."

"I don't know. We haven't been gone from home three days yet and we've spent half of what we started out with."

"Now I'll tell you to cheer up," he said, and waved his hand around. "Everything is going to be all right. Look over there in the west. It looks like the sun is going to come out. Old Pappy is running on all six cylinders. We're not going to have any more trouble."

We didn't, not for another hour. We watched as the ferry nosed in toward the slip at St. Ignace and then went down the stairs and got in the car. George turned on the ignition and pushed on the starter. We heard the grinding noise, but nothing happened. The sailor came and took off the chains and the ramp went down. The motor still hadn't started. The sailor waved for us to move. We couldn't. The big trouble was that we had been the last car to get on that ferry and now we had to be the first one to get off. No one could move until we did. The sailor came over to look down at us.

"What's the matter with that old crate?"

"I don't know," George said. "It won't start."

He kept pushing on the starter, but nothing happened. Two more sailors came sauntering over to look down.

"Try the choke," one of them said.

"This thing doesn't have any choke," George said.

"Pull down the spark. Do something!"

"I am pulling down the spark. I *am* doing something," George said.

From behind us we heard the tentative toot of a horn, then another. Three more sailors arrived. They looked menacing. More horns started tooting. From somewhere up above I heard a loud voice, I stuck my head out. The captain of the ferry was standing there with a megaphone in his hand.

"Get that goddamned piece of junk out of there," he yelled.

"I'm trying to," George said, his foot still on the starter. It seemed like all the horns on all the cars on the ferry were blowing by this time.

"All right, there," the captain shouted. "You men give him a hand there. Push him out of the way."

The six sailors got behind and began to heave. I helped. Old Pappy was a heavy car in the first place and it lacked ball bearings or something. It just didn't roll easy. Besides that, it was loaded with camping equipment and it was sitting on an incline. It didn't budge. The horns were blowing steadily now. The din was magnificent. One of the sailors straightened up from his pushing and snarled at the man in the car behind us.

"If you really want to get off this boat, stop blowing your damned horn and lend a hand here."

The man slowly climbed out the door of his car and came

forward and put his shoulder to a corner. Other doors began to open up and other men came forward. Eventually, I think, we had twenty or thirty people straining at the car. It began to move slowly up the ramp and, at long last, it rolled out onto the level dock. George steered it off to one side and all the men rubbed their hands and went back down the ramp to get back in their own cars. I looked up to see the captain, still on his bridge, shaking his fist at us.

"When you go home, go by way of Chicago," he shouted at us. "You'll never get that thing on one of these ferries again."

The cars began to come up the ramp. When the first one whirled by us, the driver rolled down his window and shouted something at us. I don't know what it was, but it was nasty. The driver of the second car off the boat did the same thing. So did the third one.

"George," I said, "we'd better get this thing out of here. These guys are just mad enough to stop and push us right off the dock into the drink. What's the matter with it anyway?"

"How the hell would I know what's the matter with it? Get some more of your goddamned underwear out of the suitcase." He gave the starter a vicious kick. There was a loud bang and a puff of blue smoke and George jumped out of there like he'd been shot.

"Hey!" I said. "The motor's running. On all six cylinders, too."

"Well, I'll be a monkey's uncle," George said. "A goddamned monkey's uncle."

We stood there looking at it while the cars rolled up out of the ramp, each driver shouting something at us as he went by.

"What do you suppose happened?" I said.

"I don't know," George said and went over and unfastened the hood. He stood there with his hand on his chin, looking down at the engine that seemed to be purring along as smoothly as anyone could wish now. He finally shook his head. "The only thing I can figure out is that the gasoline all drained back out of the carburetor when we were parked on that ramp like that. They didn't have fuel pumps on these things. They had a gravity feed. Being parked like that would do it."

We got in the car and waited until the last auto rolled up off the ferry and then George put it in gear and we rolled out through the gate and onto the streets of St. Ignace. We drove up the street for three blocks and came to a gas station and stopped and ordered the attendant to fill up the tank. While he was doing that, I suddenly remembered that I hadn't checked the wheel lugs since we left Alpena. I took the wrench and went around to the front, fitted it over a lug, and turned.

"Hey!" I yelled. "The penetrating oil has worked. This lug turned."

George came around the front of the car and took the wrench from me and tried another lug. It turned easily. So did a third one. George squatted there on his haunches and rubbed his hand over that old right front tire we had been worrying about.

"If you ask me," he said, "it was just in the nick of time." He pointed at the tire. The hole had grown to be as big as a half dollar. We could see the red tube inside the casing quite plainly. "I don't think this tire could possibly last another ten miles. Let's get it off there and put on one of the spares before we start out."

I jumped in the car and drove it over to the air hose and got out the jack. George inspected all the spares and selected one and we put it on the front wheel and blew it up. When we were all done making the change, I felt considerably better. So did George. He was grinning. To make matters even better, it was right at that moment that the sun came out. It was the first time we'd seen it since we left home.

"Everything is going to be all right for the rest of the way," he said. "I feel like celebrating."

"I know," I said. "You want a hamburger."

He nodded.

"So do I," I said. "Let's go."

We went across the street to a small diner and ordered. After I paid for the hamburgers, George's usual piece of pie à la mode, and the gas, I counted my money. We had exactly twenty-three dollars and seventy-two cents. I should have worried, but I didn't. After all, we were about to start our last leg. In just ninety more miles we would be at Germfask and Manistique Lake and our troubles would be over.

We left St. Ignace at quarter after twelve in the bright sunshine. We drove to the outskirts of town and George frowned and pointed ahead.

"A gravel road," he said.

"What did you expect in the upper peninsula?" I asked him. "Anyway, we don't have to worry. We got that tire with the hole in it off the front."

The road had been pelted by two days of rain. It was full of holes and ruts and it felt like a washboard as we bounced along. At ten minutes after one there was an earth-shaking boom and George slammed his foot on the brake pedal and fought the steering wheel until the car came to a stop.

"Which one was it?" I said.

"The right front."

I rummaged around in the back and got out the jack and walked up to the front of the car. There wasn't enough left of that tire to recognize it. It was in shreds.

"Boy, when these things blow out, they *really* blow out, don't they?" George said.

"Well, we have seven more of them."

George picked another tire out from among the spares and we put it on the wheel. When we let the jack down, however, the tire was flat.

66

"Goddamn it," George said. "Now we'll have to do it all over again."

"Aw, it's my fault, George. I forgot to blow any of them up. Get out the hand pump."

I'd pumped up bicycle tires with a hand pump when I was a kid, but it was nothing like that. I pumped and George pumped. Altogether, we spent a good half hour of good, hard backbreaking work before George said he guessed the tire was hard enough.

I looked at my watch. It was two o'clock.

"The first gas station we come to, don't forget to stop and we'll blow up the rest of those spares."

We started the car and rolled on up the road. We'd gone a little more than a mile and it was just ten minutes after two when we heard a piercing scream. It sounded a little like the zing of a bullet. George slammed his foot on the brake and fought the wheel.

"Which one was it?" I said.

"The right front again. The one we just put on there."

"This time you'd better be a little more careful about which one you pick out."

We blew up *this* tire before we put it on the wheel. It didn't seem to take quite as long. The old tire, the one that had blown out, had a hole in the side of the casing about as big as a dime.

"I don't know, but I think I can fix this one with the Monkey Tire Patch," I said. I threw the tire in the back end, intending to repair it later, and after George had started the car and we were driving up the highway I got out one of the cans and started to read the instructions. It sounded easy so I wrestled the tire around into the front seat and went to work on it as we bumped along. I had the patch on both the tube and the casing when we got our next blowout.

"Which tire was it, George?" I asked him.

"The right front. What did you think?"

67

"How far have we come, George?"

"Since St. Ignace or since the last blowout?"

"Both."

He looked at his watch. "I figure we've come about fifteen miles since the last blowout. I guess we must be thirty-five miles out of St. Ignace."

We picked another spare out of the back and pumped it up and put it on.

"Aren't there any gas stations in the upper peninsula?" George asked me, as he worked on the pump.

"Don't ask me. I've never been here before. All I've seen so far is trees."

It was four-fifteen when we finished changing that third tire. It was five o'clock when we changed the fourth one. It was also on the right front. At five-thirty we came nosing around a bend to see a gas station ahead of us. George drove in. A man came out the door rubbing his hands.

"Where's your air hose?" George asked him.

"Ain't got no air hose. How much gas you boys want?"

"We don't want any gas. All we want is some air to blow up our tires. How far is it to the next gas station."

"All depends on which way you're going."

"We're going to Germfask."

"About ten miles," the man said. "At Engadine. But he don't have no good gas. Cut-rate stuff."

"How's his air?" I asked.

"Don't know if he's got any or not. All I know is his gas ain't no good. You'd better buy some here because his station is the only other one between here and Germfask. That's thirty miles or thereabouts."

"We got enough gas," George said.

"It don't seem right your driving in here like this without buying some gas." He brightened. "Maybe you'd be interested in seeing my zoo around to the back. Cost you a nickel apiece."

"What have you got in your zoo?"

"Couple of black bear, a timber wolf, a skunk, a coon or two and a porcupine. Caught 'em all myself right here within fifty yards of the house."

"All those animals and no air," George said. "Too bad."

He put the car in gear and pulled out onto the highway. Almost immediately there was a loud bang. We changed the tire and drove on. At quarter after six we crawled into the gas station at Engadine and found an air hose. Ten minutes later we had our sixth blowout.

"By blowing up those tires, we cut down on our tire-changing time," George said.

We drove nine more miles to Blaney and turned the corner for Germfask and had our seventh blowout.

"Well, we've used up all eight of the spares," George said. "One more blowout and we're back to the old original tire with the hole in it."

"We've still got that one I put the Monkey Tire Patch on. Don't worry."

Almost as if in answer to my statement, there was a loud bang from the back of the car. I looked to find that the tire with the Monkey Tire Patch had blown out before we even got it back on the wheel.

"So much for your Monkey Tire Patch," George said, looking at the shreds.

"It couldn't be the tire patch, George. That's the only thing that's left. The rest of it is blown all to hell."

"Then it must be the air. That guy back there said the other station sold lousy gas. He is giving away lousy air, too."

It was getting dark fast by the time we moved on. We rumbled along for eight miles or more and crept up a long hill and stopped. Ahead of us, about a half mile, was a little cluster of houses. We could barely make them out in the dark.

"Well," I said. "There's Germfask. We made it."

There was a loud bang.

"Not yet, we haven't," George said. "Get out the jack. This time you'd better bring the flashlight, too. And set out that lantern up the road there so nobody runs into us while we're working."

SIX

The town of Germfask could be found on the maps of Michigan's upper peninsula, even in 1934, but I have never been able to find any gazetteer which tells anything about it. It sits on a high tableland about halfway between Lake Superior and Lake Michigan. It is a bleak, almost treeless town that is cold and cheerless under the best of circumstances. In the summer a chill wind sweeps across the plain from Lake Superior. In the winter it is buried under several feet of snow from late October until early May. It has only one street—the main road that runs from Grand Marais down to join U.S. 2 at Blaney.

When George French and I finished changing our last tire on the evening we arrived there it was pitch dark. We came down the hill into town using the beam of our flashlight to guide us on our way. We could see a few lights, but not many. The first building we came to was a two-story, square, frame affair that had a big window across the front. Behind this window there was one bulb hanging down from a cord, but there was no one in evidence despite the fact that the front door stood open. I flashed the light up at the front where there was a sign. It read "Alec MacKenzie. General Merchandise—Beer—Hotel."

I climbed down from the car and walked around and let myself in the front door. I found myself in a small grocery. There wasn't much stock on the shelves, probably not more than two hundred cans of things, but there was what I took to be a meat section off to my left and a counter stacked high with loaves of bread and a few other things of that type. At the very back of the room was an archway that opened into a darkened room. I walked over and looked in. There was a bar with a dim bulb hanging above it. There were some beer signs pasted or stenciled on the mirror, but no one was in the place. Across the bar, at the back of the room, was another door, about half open. The room behind it was brightly lit and I could hear the sound of voices so I walked over and looked in. There were two men shooting pool at a bright green table off in one corner. In the center of the room were four men seated around a card table, playing rummy. One of them, a husky man in a heavy plaid wool shirt and a florid face, looked up at me as I peeked in.

"Aye, lad," he said, "what can I do for ye?"

"I'm looking for a man named Alec MacKenzie." I gave him my name.

He put down his cards and studied me for a moment and then a broad smile crossed his face. He scraped his chair back and came around the table with both hands outstretched. He stood there pumping my hand in both of his, looking me up and down.

"Aye, laddie, ye've got the look," he said. "Ye've got the look. I should have known ye. Ah, laddie, I was verra fond of yer grandfather, verra fond." He looked me up and down again. "Yer grandfather would have made three of ye. Ah, he was a brawny man. Fought John L. Sullivan once. Did ye know that, lad?"

"No, I didn't," I said.

"Well, he did, and I was there." He dropped my hand and

put his hands on his hips. "I suppose ye've come to look over the land?"

"Yes, sir."

"Well, where do ye plan on stayin'?"

"We just got here. We haven't—"

"You go out to my camp. I'll be callin' the manager out there in a few minutes and I'll tell him ye're comin'. I wouldna have ye stay any other place."

"How far is that?" I asked.

"Eleven miles. It's out at the lake. Here—" He started to pull me toward the door.

"I'm afraid I've got a complication," I said. "We don't have any lights on our car. We're going to have to stay around here some place until morning."

He stopped and looked at me speculatively and then nodded his head vigorously. "Well, now, that's too bad, laddie, but it's na great problem." He pulled me toward the side door, and pointed. "Do ye see that light over there in the woods? That is my place. Ye go over there. Do ye have a tent?"

"Yes, sir."

"Ye can pitch it in the back yard. Ye'll find a fireplace there and plenty of wood for a fire. If ye're hungry, ye can have yerself a bite. In the mornin', when it gets light, ye can go out to the camp."

I thanked him and started to turn away, but he seemed to have a second thought.

"My granddaughter might be there. I don't know, but she might. If she is, she'll be wantin' to know who ye are and what ye're doin' there. Just tell her I sent ye." He looked me up and down again. "I was verra fond of yer grandfather, lad. Like I said, verra fond. I'm glad ye've come."

I went back out to the car and told George about my conversation. He turned around. There was a sand trail that ran along beside MacKenzie's store and we followed its twistings and turnings for about a quarter of a mile by the beam of the flashlight and eventually turned into a driveway. I helped George pull the tent out of the back of the car and then told him it might be easier if we had some light. I would find the fireplace and light a fire in it. I walked around, poking the flashlight into things until I found a big pile of firewood that seemed to run all along the back of the yard. I'd just located the little brick fireplace when a bright floodlight flashed on. It was well up on the peak of the house and brought the whole scene into clearly etched detail. Directly beneath the light a door opened and a girl stepped out onto a stair landing several feet above ground level. She stood there, trying to peer out into the yard. I walked over to a point where she could see me plainly, and where I could see her. I was quite pleased by what I saw. She was a statuesque girl, tall and broad-shouldered and she had a serenity and beauty of face that I don't think I quite expected to see up there in the north woods. She was wearing jodhpurs and a bulky, white turtle-neck sweater so that I couldn't tell very much about her figure, but from the way she stood, with her body straight and her head held high there was something almost imperial in her bearing.

I gave her my name. "Your grandfather told us we could camp out here in the back yard," I said.

She looked down at me for a moment, nodded, and then disappeared back into the house. A moment later the light went out. She hadn't said a word.

I found that a fire had already been laid in the little fireplace so I lit it and carried some more wood over and piled it on. After it was burning brightly George and I pitched our tent in front of it and went over to bring out the bacon and the other food and the cooking utensils. Everything was still wet from the previous night and we hung the blankets up near the fire so they would dry out. I held the bread up near the fire on a fork so that it would toast and be less soggy. The meal tasted very good. When we were done with it, and had put the things away, we simply crawled into bed. I think we were both pretty tired from all that tire changing we had done. Just before we went to sleep, I asked George if he had seen the girl.

"Yeah, I saw her," he said. "I don't like her looks. She looks pretty stuck up to me and I don't like stuck-up girls."

"That's funny. That's just the way I like them. It's lots more fun cutting them down to size."

"You aren't going to cut that one down to size. She don't even know you're alive."

We woke up at the first light of dawn. I poked up the fire and made us some coffee and fried up some more of the bacon. We pulled down the tent and tucked everything away in the back of the car. There wasn't any sign of life in the house so I suggested we walk over and take a look at Germfask. There wasn't much to it. When we got over to the main road we counted eight buildings, and that included the house we had just come from. There were two store buildings right next to each other. One of them was that combination general store, bar and hotel that belonged to Alec MacKenzie. The other contained a lunch counter and a store that advertised "Sporting Goods." Next to the sporting goods store was a little square box of a place that had a sign over its door that read "United States Post Office, Germfask, Mich." About fifty yards up the road from that was a white clapboard house with a wide lawn around it. Across the street from the house was a brightly painted red barn with several pieces of farm equipment in front of it. Almost directly across from the post office was a church. It, too, was painted white, and it had a steeple of sorts. The only other building in the town was a long, one-story affair that was covered with tar paper. It was nudged into the corner of a road intersection almost opposite MacKenzie's store. There was a flagpole in front of it and a sign over the door that read "United States of America. Headquarters, Civilian Conservation Corps Battalion No. 4322." I didn't

75

know it at the time, of course, but that little road running off at right angles to the main highway was a logging road that had been built fifty years before.

George and I wandered around this little town, stopping to look up at each building as we came to it. There wasn't a soul in sight and not a single car had passed up and down the road in the half hour or more it took us to walk over there and look the place over. We sauntered on back over to Alec MacKenzie's house and walked all the way around it. It was quite different than anything else in the whole village. To begin with, it had trees. It sat on a little elevation and all around it were towering pines. There must have been fifty of them. We didn't know it, but these were the last remaining remnants of those magnificent Michigan pines which had once made the state famous. The house, itself, was different. From the outside it resembled a log cabin, yet it wasn't. It was two stories high and all along the lower level, both front and rear, there were big windows, almost picture windows, that looked out over the landscape. At one end of the house was a garage wide enough to take two cars. It took me a little while to realize that I was looking at a very luxurious place. It was the kind of hunting lodge that a wealthy man would build for himself in the wilderness. Everything about it indicated that it had meticulous care. The back yard, when we got around to looking at it again, proved to be a level area with a stone wall around it. It was sand—the whole area around Germfask was sandy soil—and it had been carefully raked over. It looked like it had been manicured. The only marks on it were those made by George and me when we camped out there. Even the woodpile was neat and exactly in line.

"It's too bad we don't have a rake," George said. "I feel guilty about mussing this place up."

"Maybe if we looked we could find one," I said.

"I don't guess we'd better go rummaging around now,"

George said, and pointed up at one of the chimneys on the house. Smoke was coming out of it.

I went up the back steps and knocked on the door that the girl had come out of the night before. After a moment, it swung open and Alec MacKenzie stood there.

"Morning, lads. Come in and have a sip of coffee with me."

Inside, the house was more luxurious than it was outside. There was one big room with a thirty-foot-high, raftered ceiling, all finished in knotty pine. Around the whole room ran a balcony and off the balcony doors opened into bedrooms. The furniture was the kind that one would expect to find in a hunting lodge, made out of what appeared to be small logs or limbs of trees, but polished and smoothed until it shone. Animal pelts of all kinds hung from the walls. Indian blankets hung from the railing of the balcony. There were several bearskin rugs on the floor. A large fireplace occupied almost all of one end of the room, or so it seemed to me. A bright, cheerful fire burned in it and Alec Mac-Kenzie led us over to take a seat facing it. After he poured the coffee he leaned back and folded his hands over his stomach.

"Let me tell ye about yer grandfather, laddie," he said. "When I come over here from the old country in '78, I went to work for him down below. He was the first boss I ever had, and the only one. Ye wouldna know it by lookin' at me, but I'm eighty-six years old. In those days I was a fair stout lad, but yer grandfather was a better man. In those days the man who could whip everyone else in the camp was the boss and that's why yer grandfather was the boss. He was a fair boss, too, and I worked for him for six years. When he come up here in '82 I come along with him, me and his brother Tom who was only eighteen then." He droned on for a few minutes about what it was like to work in the logging camps. Then he got up and went over to a desk at the other end of the room and brought back a big map which he unrolled on the coffee table. "Now, lad, let's take a look at

this property of yer grandfather's. This is Big Manistique
Lake, which ye'll be seein' shortly. Yer grandfather's property runs from this point all along the north shore of the
lake, to here." He pointed as he went along. "It runs north
to the county line. In some cases it's a half mile deep. In
other places it is considerably less, but it's the lake frontage
that's important these days. It's not been worth much these
fifty years or more because it's scrubland. Ye can't grow
anything on it, and there just isn't verra much ye *can* do
with it."

"I don't understand why Grandfather ever bought it, or
when?"

"Well, that's a long story, lad. When we finished loggin'
off the land around the lake in '84, yer grandfather went
back down to the lower peninsula. He had a job down there
the next winter. Yer Uncle Tom and me liked this country
up here and we wanted to stay. There was another man
worked in yer grandfather's camp who wanted to stay too.
He was John Fuller. All of us liked that lake. It's the best
lake in the upper peninsula and when the logging operations were through we went to the lumber company and
offered to buy it. What we was doin' was buyin' the whole
lake. With the timber cut off it, it wasn't worth much. The
lumber company had already run a survey to see if there
was any iron on it and there wasn't. So they sold it to us
cheap. Yer Uncle Tom didn't have any money though, so
yer grandfather put up his share—three hundred dollars, I
think it was. Well, yer Uncle Tom never got married and
he never paid back the three hundred dollars, either. When
he died in '98, it just went to yer grandfather."

"If it wasn't worth anything, why did he keep it all these
years?"

Alec MacKenzie smiled. "Yer grandfather was a stubborn
man, laddie, verra stubborn. I had something to do with it,
though. When yer Uncle Tom and Fuller and I bought that
land, we had a company. We had some ideas what we

wanted to do with it. There was some idea speculatin', and some idea of cuttin' second growth off it. It don't make much difference now. Fuller was a hard man to get along with and yer grandfather didn't like him. He tried to keep yer Uncle Tom from goin' into the deal, but yer Uncle Tom was stubborn, too. Anyway, after yer Uncle Tom died, yer grandfather and Fuller couldn't get along at all and so we broke up the land company and split up the land. We drew lots to see who would get what. I got the south shore of the lake. Yer grandfather got the north shore and Fuller got both ends. We thought we had the best of it, but ye never can tell about those things. In 1900, some rich folks from Chicago come up here and bought all that land south of here where Blaney is now. They were figurin' on build-ing a nice big huntin' and fishin' lodge down there. Private club. They did, too. It's quite a place, as you'll see when you look at it. They got a big lodge, golf links, swimming pool, everything. Real nice little rich man's toy. Anyway, when they were planning it, Manistique Lake was part of the original layout. If yer goin' to have a huntin' and fishin' club, ye got to have a place to fish and that lake is the best in this part of the world. They had some snoopers up here lookin' at it. One of them run across John Fuller who was livin' out there at the lake. He found out that Fuller owned part of the lake frontage, but not the rest. When he tried to find out who owned the rest Fuller wouldn't tell him. Fuller just told him he'd get all the land together and sell the whole thing to the Chicago people for twenty thousand dollars. The first thing I heard about it was when Fuller come over to the Soo and offered me six hundred dollars for my part of the land. He wrote your grandfather and offered him three hundred dollars for his. That Fuller was a sharp man, I'll tell you. Well, I'm pretty good at snoopin' myself and I got wind of what was up. I told yer grand-father and I told him what I thought the land would be worth to these people. I offered it to them for fifty thousand dollars. It was supposed to be split twenty-five thousand apiece to yer grandfather and me. I didn't care what Fuller got for his. I was wrong. I guess I was too greedy. They didn't buy, but I figured they'd come around eventually and I told yer grandfather so. That's one of the reasons he hung onto it all these years. In the meantime, Fuller couldn't sell his property, either, but he was a mean cuss. He made another little deal with those land people. He rented out fishing rights on the lake to them and, just to keep the lake nice and private the way those fellows wanted it, he blocked off the old logging road so that nobody but the Blaney people and him could use it. That was the only way you could get into the lake in those days. For twelve years yer grandfather and I couldn't even get into our own property. I finally got the state to build a road up to Curtis in 1919 so I could get into my property, but up until the present moment, there's been no road built into the north shore."

"It's still worthless then?"

He sat up and picked up his coffee cup and sat looking into the fire for a moment. "I'll not fool ye, lad, I have an interest in acquirin' that property. If I was to have the ownership of it, I might be able to develop it. Mind ye, I say I *might* be able to develop it. It would take a considerable amount of money and time to do it and there aren't verra many as can manage such a project. I wouldna try it if I didna think this Depression wasn't going to end some day. I see ye walkin' over there to have a look at the town. Ye didna find much there, did ye?"

"No, sir," I said.

"Ye'll be surprised when people start stirrin' and ye have another look at it. There's money to be made up here, even in these times, and I'm thinkin' it will get better, but I'll be frank wi' ye. There's a lot of ifs about this property of yer grandfather's. I might be able to develop it and I might not, but right now my main interest is keepin' it in friendly hands. I wouldna want it to fall into the hands of Charlie Fuller.

I think I'd be willin' to pay a good price to see that it didn't."

"Charlie Fuller?"

"Aye. Old John passed on fifteen years ago and Charlie's his son. If ye have the misfortune to meet him, ye'll not like him. He's tight with a penny and sharp with a dollar and about as devious a man as ever lived. His father was a scoundrel before him, but he wasn't any worse than Charlie. When he finds out yer grandfather has passed on, he'll be after that property and ye may depend on it. Yer grandfather would have no dealin's with him and I'm hopin' ye'll not."

"My brothers and I haven't made up our mind what we're going to do with it yet," I said. "I rather imagine we'll sell it, but the reason I came up here was to look it over and see just what there is to it. Right now, my friend George here and I are going to camp out on it for a few weeks."

Alec MacKenzie's eyes twinkled and he rubbed his chin. "Laddie, I don't think ye'll be very happy tryin' to camp on that property. Ye'll find there are a few drawbacks, not the least of which is the fact that ye cannot get into it unless ye have a boat. Now ye take my advice. I have a huntin' and fishin' camp out on the south shore. I'll call my manager out there and tell him who ye are. He'll let you have a boat and whatever else ye need. Ye be my guests."

"Do you think you could show us around?"

"I'd be happy to, but I'm afeerd it will have to wait for a few days. I'm leavin' this mornin' to go down to Lansing to see the governor. Funny thing, I was goin' to drop by Flint to see yer father, but I won't have to now. There's no hurry about this. After I get Mr. Comstock straightened out, I'll be back. About a week or ten days dependin' what I run into down there. This is state election year, you know, and I'm sort of runnin' things for the Democrats up here in the upper peninsula." He bent over the map again. "Now pay close attention while I tell ye how to get out to my camp.

In the old days, ye'd have had to drive all the way back down through Blaney and up through Curtis, more'n thirty mile, but since the CCs built the new road across the swamp it's only about nine miles. Ye'll find a road runnin' off the highway over there next to the CC barracks. That's the old loggin' road yer grandfather built for the lumber company in the summer of '82. Ye just follow it due east. Ye won't have no trouble because there's no way to get off it anyway. When ye get almost to the lake, ye come to a road runnin' off to the right. It's not here on this map. The CCs just built it this last year. It comes out right in front of my camp. Mind ye, now, ye have to be verra careful not to miss the turn. There are no signs to mark the way. Every time I put one up, Charlie Fuller takes it down. He is just about the orneriest cuss as God ever put on this earth."

We all got up and Alec MacKenzie led us over to the back door to let us out. As we stood there saying good-by, I saw the girl come running up the front steps, across the room from us. She let herself in the front door and waved airily at her grandfather and he waved back. Then she ducked up a set of stairs, padded along the balcony, and disappeared into an open door. I suppose the most remarkable part of this was the fact that she was clad only in a black, one-piece bathing suit. She was really built. I felt like whistling. Actually, I did whistle when I got outside.

"Boy," I said to George, "did you see that?"

"I saw it," George said grimly, "and you can forget it. You couldn't get to first base with her."

We got in our car and backed out of the driveway to follow the little sand trail over to the highway. Alec Mac-Kenzie was right about the town. When we'd walked around it earlier, there hadn't been anyone in sight. Now there were fifteen or twenty cars parked on the street. People seemed to be bustling in and out of the stores and the post office. Others were standing beside their cars, trying out their fishing casts or checking through their equipment kits. Two men were standing in front of the sporting goods store, going over a map. Almost to a man, all these people were wearing waders and had bright-colored flies hanging from their hats.

"Boy," George said, "this looks like the fishing capital of the universe."

The old logging road was narrow, but it was graveled and in excellent condition. We only met two cars in the whole length of it and each time we had to slow down and maneuver carefully to get by. There were no turnoffs at all. I think that we passed just three houses and all of them resembled run-down shacks. There didn't seem to be anyone living in them. In the front yards of two of them were broken-down old cars with tires and window glass missing.

"I don't know whether this is just the Depression or whether this is just the natural state of things," I said, "but this sure looks like a pretty poor part of the world."

"If people just go off and leave their houses and land like this, I don't think your grandfather's property is worth very much," George said. "If he offers you twenty-five dollars, you'd better take it."

We'd driven a little over six miles when we came to a road that turned off the one we were on and ran to the right. We stopped and looked at it. It was unimproved, rutted, and narrow. It looked more like a cowpath than a road. Off in the distance about a quarter of a mile we could see water. It looked to me like the road ran right down into it. Ahead of us stretched the gravel road, as good as ever.

"God," George said, "that can't be the road Mr. Mac-Kenzie was talking about, can it?"

"I don't think so," I said. "He said it was a new road and I'm pretty sure the CCC boys could build a better road than that. Drive on a little ways and let's see what we come to."

A slight hill loomed just ahead of us and the gravel road seemed to run into a thick woods. George put the car in low gear and we labored up to the top of the hill, dipped down over the other side, made a sharp turn to the left, another sharp turn to the right, and then began a long steady climb. The pine woods closed in around us and we seemed to be passing through the forest primeval. It was deep green and absolutely beautiful, but no roads turned off ours in either direction and there wasn't room enough to turn around. Suddenly, in the midst of this wilderness, we came to a small rustic arch that spanned the road. Printed on it in big yellow letters was the legend "Fuller's Camp." I looked at George and he looked at me and the next thing I knew we emerged from the woods and rolled out onto a broad, green lawn. The road had just disappeared. On our right was a big, three-story house of white clapboard. Ahead of us, scattered about the lawn were cars and tents. This whole common was perhaps fifty yards wide and a hundred yards long. It ended in a high bluff that looked out over a large, deep, blue body of water. At my first glimpse of it, I thought that Manistique Lake was the most beautiful lake I'd ever seen. George had stopped the car, of course, and we sat there for several moments taking in the scene. George stirred himself.

"I guess we'd better get out of here and get back to that other road," George said.

"Yeah, I guess it would be a good idea."

We'd stopped on the very crown of a hill. Ahead of us the ground seemed fairly level, but behind us, and to either side, the grass sloped away rather sharply into the woods from which we had just emerged. George put the car in reverse to turn around. In order to make the turn around he had to back down onto the slope so that when he came to a stop, the radiator was tilted upward at a rather sharp angle. The ground was firm enough to support the car, but that grass was slippery. George shifted routinely from reverse into low and let out the clutch, then pulled on the gas lever. The back wheels spun on the slippery grass. It was just one strain too many for those old tires that had carried us the four hundred miles from home. The tire on the left rear blew out with a large bang. At almost the same time, the tire on the right rear let go with a piercing whistle that sounded like a ricocheting bullet. The very flatness of those two tires gave us the extra added traction that one needed on a slippery slope like that. The car suddenly lurched forward and then there was a horrible rending, grinding noise in the rear end. The car seemed to go dead and hang there for a moment. Then, slowly, and despite the fact that the motor was still running and despite the fact that the car was still in low gear, we began to roll backward. I knew that something was wrong and I instinctively reached down and grabbed the emergency brake and we stopped rolling. The two of us sat there for a moment and George heaved a big sigh. Both of us got out slowly and walked around to the back and bent over. I think I actually expected to see blood gushing from a wound. I couldn't see a thing. I straightened up and took a step and bumped into a man. He was a handsome man, broad of face with hair graying at the temples. He was grinning at me.

"You boys got trouble?" he said.

"*Something's* wrong," George said, looking up. "I don't know what it is."

"You couldn't have picked a better place to break down," the man said. "I'm Charlie Fuller."

We were in the clutches of the enemy.

SEVEN

It seems reasonable to talk about Charlie Fuller's admirable traits for a moment. On the surface he seemed to typify all the virtues in which Americans had set store for generations. He'd been born in a log cabin not a hundred yards from where we first saw him. In his whole life he had never traveled more than fifty miles from that site. His father ran a little sawmill on the property and I think that over the years he had furnished the lumber for most of the houses in the area, but old John Fuller was a product of the horse-and-buggy age. At the time he died in 1919 the real automobile age was just beginning in the upper peninsula, and his son, Charlie, understood what it meant. With people able to travel there would be people coming. At that time the upper peninsula was one of the best hunting and fishing areas in the world. It was famous for that and now, for the first time, people could take advantage of it. During his younger years Charlie had acted as a paid guide for the rich men down in Blaney and he was undoubtedly the best guide in that whole area. It was said of him that he knew every fish in the upper peninsula by its first name and that he knew exactly where and when each buck would be going to water.

When he inherited the property on Manistique Lake from his father his first act was to open a hunting and fishing camp of his own on the bluffs that overlooked the west end of the lake. He had started out by building the imposing-looking white clapboard house where the log cabin stood. It had room for twelve guests and his family. In the years that followed he had built eleven cabins of two or three bedrooms. Usually he would start one each fall. He also had a barn, an icehouse and the old sawmill. He had a dock that ran out into the lake for a hundred feet, a boathouse, and more than fifty boats of assorted shapes and sizes. The remarkable thing about all this is that he built all these things with his own hands. He sawed the lumber in his mill from timber he cut down. He did the carpentry work and the bricklaying and the plumbing. There was nothing that Charlie Fuller could not do, from the dirtiest jobs to the bookkeeping. And there was nothing he didn't do, for the most admirable trait of all was his sheer love of hard work. At the time I first knew him he had worked from dawn until well into the night for fifteen years. He never had an idle moment. If he had a few minutes he would run over to his newest cabin and nail on a few more boards. He built a dairy herd. He kept two or three hundred chickens. He butchered his own pigs and smoked his own meat. In the long winter months when he was snowed in and cut off from the world he cut the ice in the lake and stored it in his icehouse, or worked in his basement painting and calking his boats, or put the finishing touches on the cabin he had started that year. At some time in the early 1920s he got married and over the years he had three daughters. He put his wife to work. He put his mother-in-law to work, and as fast as they became capable of toddling around, he put his daughters to work. By 1934, Charlie Fuller's camp stood as a monument to industry and hard work. Other people copied and emulated him, notably Alec MacKenzie, by building hunting and fishing camps of their own, but none were as successful or as up-to-date as Charlie's.

All this should have made Charlie a respected and admired citizen of his area, but it didn't, for Charlie had a peculiar streak in him. He had a bad reputation. Where it came from, I don't know. He may have inherited it, or he may have been taught it, but whatever the case, he never missed a chance to take advantage of people. He was suspicious of everyone and it was the cardinal principle of his life to get what he could out of people before they got what they could out of him. Hardly anyone within a radius of forty miles had not been victimized at some time by Charlie. As a result, they stayed just as far away from him as they could. Long before I ever saw Germfask, Charlie had become *persona non grata* there. Even the postmistress refused to let him in her place. His mail and mail for the guests at his camp were addressed to Manistique, forty miles away, and once a week Mrs. Fuller would drive all the way over there and pick it up. When the CCC boys opened the new road across the swamp and Charlie had access to the town of Curtis, he might have been able to use it as a substitute for Germfask, but he knew better than to go there for he had long since worn out his welcome there. Even in the days when he could only get there by boat, he had managed to alienate everyone.

The guests at Charlie's camp did not have a much higher opinion of him than his neighbors, yet they came back year after year and sent their friends there. There were only two possible explanations. The first was unquestionably his reputation as the best guide. The fishermen who stayed at his camp were practically guaranteed messes of any kind of fish they could ask for. If you wanted bass, Charlie sent you where the bass were biting. If you wanted trout, Charlie knew where they were at any given hour of the day. The hunters who came north in the fall always went home with a buck. If they wanted a bear, Charlie would get them a bear. And, as I said, his camp was up-to-date. The cabins were comfortable and clean. For those guests who stayed in the hotel—or the big house—the food was reputed to be the best in the upper peninsula. The place was run efficiently.

Charlie's bitterest enemy was Alec MacKenzie. Along with the property, Charlie had inherited the bitter feud that had begun twenty years before. Neither he nor MacKenzie expected or gave any quarter. It was MacKenzie's fondest wish to drive Charlie out of business and in that summer I arrived there, MacKenzie was in the process of building a new and modern camp which was calculated to attract all the disgruntled guests away from Fuller's Camp. I sensed a little of this in the tone of Alec MacKenzie's voice as he talked about Charlie. During that ride George and I took along the old logging road I had some small doubts as to whether this man was as much an ogre as MacKenzie made him out. When I saw him for the first time, I was convinced that Charlie was a good fellow. He was a rugged man, built like a fullback. Everything about him exuded strength. He was fifty years old that summer and the years of hard work and sacrifice had hardly left a mark upon him. He certainly was not a person to alarm anyone. The smile that he directed at us seemed open and frank. Unfortunately, you never knew Charlie for more than five minutes without finding out about him. On that morning he bent over and looked under our crippled old car.

"It don't look like you're going to get it fixed very soon, does it?" he said, and straightened up to wave his hand around the big common. "Well, boys, you can camp right here while you work on it. We've got everything you can possibly need, right here. You can pick out one of those fireplaces there and pitch your tent next to it. Over there you can see that building. It has showers—hot and cold running water—and lavatories. Modern in every detail. Over here at the big house we got a store where you can buy anything you need. Down there at the lake you'll find plenty of boats in case you want to go fishing. The whole business will cost you ten dollars a week—in advance."

"Ten dollars a week is a lot of money," I said. "We can't afford it."

"Ain't very much you can do about it," Charlie said. "Don't look to me like you're going to be able to move that thing."

"It don't look to me like there's very much you can do about it, either," I said. "We just don't have ten dollars."

The smile disappeared from his face. I thought he was going to bare his fangs.

"Well, now, ain't that a pretty situation? What did you come here for if you didn't have no money."

"We didn't intend to come here at all. We must have missed the turn in the road down below there. We were told there would be signs, but somebody must have taken them down."

"What kind of signs?"

"Road signs. It's against the law to take down road signs. I'm going to report it to the state police."

"Believe me, boy, there weren't no road signs down there. Nothing but billboards that was cluttering up the scenery." The smile slowly came back to his face. "Now, I don't want no trouble here, boys. I'm easy to get along with as you'll find out. Tell you what I'll do. I got another camping area over there in the woods. Ain't as good as this one up here on the common. Ain't as much sun and you got to walk farther to get to the lavatory and you have to use a common fireplace. It will cost you five dollars a week, and of course you'll have to move the car yourself. If I move it I'll have to charge you five dollars."

"Why?"

"Gas for my truck. Besides, my time is valuable."

"Look, mister," George said, "didn't you ever hear of the good Samaritan? We're in trouble and we told you we don't have much money. All we want to do is get this car fixed and get it out of here. Right now we're not interested whether a place is convenient or not. We just want a place where we can stay until we get this work done. It shouldn't take us very long."

He scowled at us. "I don't see why two good-for-nothing kids would go running around the country in an old wreck like that without money. Ought to have more sense." He heaved a big sigh and pointed down into the woods behind the car. "There's a picnic table down there and an outhouse. If you want to you can camp down there in the woods. Cost you a dollar and a half."

I looked the place over from up there on the hill. I couldn't see anything the matter with it. "All right," I said, "we'll stay down there."

"In advance," he said, grimly.

I reached in my pocket and pulled out a dollar bill and two quarters and handed it to him.

"All right," he said. "Just remember, I don't want to catch you two up here on the common or using the lavatory. That's reserved for my quality guests. You can get your water over there behind the barn. You'll find a spring over there. Now get this old pile of junk back down there in the woods out of sight. It ain't good for business up here where everyone can see it." He turned his back on us and stalked off toward the house. George glowered at his receding back.

"He is a son of a bitch," he said.

"I don't like him any better than you do, George," I said. "But it's not going to do us any good to stand around and call him names. We don't have much choice. What do you suppose is the matter with this thing?"

"I hate to tell you what I think, but I don't know for sure. I won't know until I take it apart. Let's go down and see what kind of a place we got to live in."

We walked down to the picnic table and began rummaging around. I'm not sure what the most important thing was, but George found a pile of old fence posts.

"We can use those to put under the rear end," he said. "We'll jack it up and put the logs under it and I'll pull the wheels and take the housing off the rear axle. While I'm doing that, you'd better fix those tires."

We hacked a little path down into the woods and then George went up and released the emergency brake and steered the car as it rolled down into the woods. It came to rest about twenty feet from the picnic table. We had a small cleared area about twenty feet square in which to live and work. All around us were thick woods and tangled undergrowth. It was about the time George climbed down out of the driver's seat that we discovered our second most important thing.

"Well, I know why he let this place go for a dollar and a half," George said.

"Why?"

"If you haven't found out yet, you soon will. We've stolen the mosquitoes' home. My God, I never saw them so thick and so big. This must be some kind of a swamp down here."

By mutual consent, we turned our attention to the car first. It seemed important that we get it fixed and get out of there. While George jacked the rear end up, I carried fence posts and slid them under it. Within a half hour we had both back wheels six inches off the ground and the rear axle was resting on a substantial platform. I took the two back tires off and went to work with the tire patch. George began the task of removing the bolts on the rear axle housing. We weren't half done before we had to stop.

"We've got to do something about these mosquitoes," George said. "They're driving me out of my mind."

"What do we do?"

"We'll build a smudge. Get all the grass and leaves you can."

We built four smudges so that no matter which way the wind blew some of the smoke would blow toward the car where we were working. It helped keep some of the mosquitoes away, but working in the middle of the smudge was almost as bad as working in the mosquitoes. We both coughed and sneezed and stopped to wipe the tears out of our eyes. I kept working away with the Monkey Tire Patch and eventually got the tubes back in the tires and began pumping them up with the hand pump. To my great gratification they held air nicely. At least that part of the repair operation seemed to be a success. We weren't so lucky on the other thing. George got the axle housing off and began reaching his hand in to feel around. About the time I finished pumping up the last tire he came over to me holding up a circular piece of steel.

"What's that?" I asked.

"That is the ring gear. It's the circular gear that fits on the end of the drive shaft and connects with the rear axle and drives the wheels. All but three of the teeth have been sheared off it. I couldn't have done a better job with a chisel."

"What do we do?"

"There's only one thing we can do. Get a new one."

"Where do we find it?"

He held out his hands in a helpless gesture. "I don't know. Maybe from the Buick factory, but if we couldn't find a valve or tires for a 1916 car, I don't think we're likely to find a ring gear. Our best bet is probably a junk yard, but I don't remember seeing a single junk yard all the way up here from St. Ignace. There's two possible things we can do. We can write everybody we know at home and ask them to go out and look for one in the junk yards around there, or I can scout around here and see if I can find a machine shop where I can make one or have one made."

"That will cost money, George."

"No matter how you look at it, it's going to cost money.

If we have to stay here very long it's going to cost money or if we have one made it's going to cost money. Right now I guess the cheapest thing to do is write letters and get everybody started to looking."

"All right. I guess we're stuck here for a little while, anyway. Let's make a camp and eat something and then start writing letters."

We pitched our tent and dug a pit for our fire and I got the food out of the back and cooked us some supper. I hadn't bought very much food in the beginning and that evening meal finished off the last of our bacon and bread. After I'd washed up the dishes and put things away, I talked to George about it.

"I think I'd better go up to the store and buy some things," I said. "He said he had everything we'd need up there."

"Go ahead," George said. "I'll stay down here and write letters."

I walked up on the front steps of the big house and in through the front door. I found myself in a little room about ten feet square. There were shelves all around it, but there wasn't much on them. There was a can of beans on one shelf and a couple of cans of soup on another shelf. Charlie Fuller was standing behind the counter.

"I thought you said you had a store here."

He waved his arm around the room. "You're in it," he said.

"You don't have very much to sell."

"I guess I can take care of the likes of you. What you don't see, just ask for it. If I ain't got it, I'll get it for you. My wife goes over to Manistique every Friday and does the shopping. What do you want?"

"You got any bread?"

"Yep."

"I'll take a loaf," I said.

"Don't sell it by the loaf. Sell it by the slice. How many slices do you want?"

I did some mental arithmetic and told him I'd take eight slices. "How about bacon?" I asked. "Do you sell bacon?"

"How many slices?" he asked.

"Ten slices."

He pulled out a drawer under the counter and counted out the slices of bread, then went over to a refrigerator, opened it, and counted out the slices of bacon. He wrapped the whole thing in an old newspaper and shoved it across the counter to me. "That will be sixty-six cents," he said.

"Sixty-six cents?" I asked. "That sounds like a lot of money for that little bit. How much do you get for a slice of bread?"

"Two cents a slice."

"How much for the bacon?"

"Five cents a slice."

I got out a pencil and did some figuring on the margin of the newspaper.

"As near as I can figure out, you're getting about forty cents a loaf for bread and a dollar a pound for bacon," I said.

"If you say so, I guess maybe that's right."

"I know, Mr. Fuller, but you can buy bread for ten cents a loaf anyplace, and I just bought bacon for twenty-four cents a pound."

He pointed his finger at me. "Now look here, son, I didn't ask you to come in here and buy anything from me, but as long as you're in here, you pay my prices. If you don't want to, that's all right with me." He reached out for the package on the counter.

"Never mind," I said, and took the change out of my pocket and counted out sixty-six cents.

"Figured you'd pay it," he said. "You ain't got much choice."

I walked back down to the tent, still turning the meaning of this over in my mind. George was sitting there at the picnic table by the light of the lantern, brushing mosquitoes and smudge away with one hand, writing letters with the other.

"This is an expensive place," I said, and told him about the bread and bacon.

"The sooner you get busy writing letters to people to get that ring gear, the sooner we'll get out of here," he said, somewhat impatiently.

I sat down across from him and drew up the tablet and started writing. I wrote ten letters, altogether. One to my father and the rest to various friends. I exhorted them all to go out immediately to the various junk yards in the area and look for a ring gear for a 1916 Buick. Long before I'd finished these letters, George had finished his and had left them lying on the table. He had crawled into the tent and pulled down the mosquito netting and had gone to sleep.

We got up at dawn the next morning and ate our usual breakfast of bacon and toast and coffee and about seven o'clock I scooped the twenty letters up off the picnic table and trudged up to Charlie Fuller's store. Charlie was standing behind the counter, picking his teeth. Being a city boy, I think I expected to find a mailbox up there and I know I expected him to have stamps. I asked him for twenty three-cent ones. He opened a drawer and took out a sheet and tore off the twenty and shoved them across the counter. I took the rest of my loose change out of my pocket and counted out sixty cents and put it down beside the stamps.

"That ain't enough," he said.

"What do you mean, it's not enough?" I asked him. "Three times twenty is sixty cents."

"I get six cents apiece for them stamps."

"But you can't do that," I sputtered. "You can't make a profit on postage stamps. It's against the law."

"Not so's I've heard, it ain't. Now, son, you looky here. My wife has to go all the way over to Manistique to get them stamps and I get six cents apiece for them."

"I suppose you charge another three cents apiece for carrying them over there and putting them in the mailbox."

"Well, not exactly, but I do get two cents apiece."

"Eight cents apiece for mailing a letter? Whoever heard of such a thing?"

He made a face. "Son, I'm tired of you complaining about my prices. You just ain't in very much of a position to complain, either. Your trouble is that you ain't got much choice. Either take it or leave it."

"I'll be goddamned if I'll pay them," I said.

He brought up his finger and shook it at me. "That will be enough of that swearing," he said. "I don't allow no swearing in this camp. I got three young daughters to bring up here."

EIGHT

I was really fuming when I stalked back into the camp. I told George about the bacon and the bread and the stamps. To my surprise he didn't seem to be upset at all. He just went around poking up the smudge fires.

"The funny thing about it is that he's right," George said, when I'd finished spouting off. "Just what the hell are you going to do about it? You've got to mail those letters. If you don't mail them, how do you expect us to find a ring gear and get this car fixed? And where else are you going to get anything to eat?"

"In Germfask," I said.

"And just how the hell do you expect to get to Germfask? It's seven miles to Germfask and our car is busted down."

"I'll hitchhike if I can. If I can't hitchhike, I'll walk. I'm just not going to stand still and let him gouge us. Are you coming with me or are you going to stay here with the mosquitoes?"

He looked around. "I guess I'll come with you."

We walked. We walked every foot of that seven miles into Germfask. We got there a little before noon. In that whole seven miles we saw only one car. It was a shiny little

Ford sports roadster and it went by us in a cloud of dust without the slightest indication that the driver had even seen us as we waved and gestured frantically to be picked up. The driver of the car was MacKenzie's granddaughter. George looked after her as she disappeared up the road.

"I guess that will show you what kind of a dame she is," he said. "She didn't even slow down."

"Maybe she didn't recognize us," I said, somewhat lamely.

"Of course, she didn't recognize us, but that shouldn't have anything to do with it. Most people would have stopped and picked up a couple of fellows like us whether they knew us or not. She's got a hard and stony heart."

We got the stamps in Germfask, and mailed the letters, being careful to write our return address on all the envelopes as "General Delivery, Germfask, Mich." After we finished our business at the post office, we went into Alec MacKenzie's store where I bought a loaf of bread and two pounds of bacon. Neither one was much of a bargain. The bread was twenty cents a loaf and the bacon was forty cents a pound. Even at those figures it was better than doing business with Charlie Fuller. Quite naturally, I sat down and counted my money afterward. We were down to nineteen dollars and ninety-six cents. It was only Thursday afternoon. We'd been gone from home for less than a week. As we straggled along toward home, I spent a lot of time pointing all this out to George. He endured it until we reached the halfway point in our walk and then he sat down obstinately on a rock and refused to move another step.

"I'm tired of getting a treasurer's report every time you spend a nickel," he said. "I'm not going to listen to any more of this crap."

"I know, George, but it's bad. You don't seem to realize that."

"Well, why don't we do something about it, then, instead of talking about it all the time?"

"You got any ideas?"

"Sure. When we came up here we were going to camp out on your grandfather's property. Let's get the hell to doing it. If we get started catching fish, and if we get away from old man Fuller, maybe we'll stop spending money and maybe I'll get some peace."

I looked at him in some surprise. I hadn't realized that I'd sort of lost track of what we had started out to do.

"I guess you're right," I said. "Tomorrow morning we'll go over to Grandfather's property and pick out a good camping spot and move over there."

We walked along toward home talking about this and finally George scratched his head.

"I guess that takes care of us, but I just happened to think. What are we going to do about the car? We can't just leave it there in Fuller's camp. He'll keep right on charging us rent for it. We could run up quite a bill for that. When it gets up to around twenty-five dollars he could sue you and take all the property away from you."

"God, I hadn't thought of *that*," I said. It was my turn to sit down on a rock. "What do we do, George?"

"To begin with, I don't think you'd better tell Fuller what your name is. Just keep your mouth shut."

"Don't worry about that. I won't say a thing, and don't you say anything, either. What else we going to do?"

"Well, I heard Mr. MacKenzie say he was willing to pay a good price to keep that property from falling into Fuller's hands. Maybe we ought to go and tell him that Fuller is going to sue you and take that property away from you if we don't get that car out of there. I'll bet he'd get a tow truck over there and get it in a hurry. He could haul the car over to his place and park it there until the ring gear comes. Then we wouldn't have any worries at all."

"Mr. MacKenzie isn't here. He's gone down to Lansing to see the governor. He won't be back until next week."

"Well, we're not in any hurry. The rent's paid up until

next Wednesday. While we're waiting we can go over and pick out the camping place."

We finished our walk home. It was getting along toward seven o'clock in the evening by the time we got there so we just cooked up some supper and turned in so we could get an early start the next morning.

We were up at daylight that Friday morning. The only thing we decided to take along with us was our fishing poles in case we ran across any nice-looking fishing places. As we walked out of our camp I remembered that I'd seen a map of the lake hanging from the wall in Fuller's store so I suggested to George that we stop and take a look at it before we started out. There was a frumpy-looking little woman sweeping out behind the counter when we came through the front door. She stopped and leaned on her broom to watch us when we walked over to the map.

"You boys going fishing?" she asked us.

"I guess so," I said, without turning around.

"Did you make arrangements with Charlie for a boat?"

I turned around to look at her. "We weren't planning to use any boat."

"Well, you won't catch any fish in this lake without any boat. They don't come in anywhere near shore. I'm Charlie's wife, and I ought to know. Of course, you could be going trout fishing. That's a different thing. The best trout fishing, right now, is over on the Taquahmenon River. That's about thirty miles from here, on the road to Newberry." She cocked her head and studied us for a moment. "Say, ain't you two the boys with the broken-down car? How you going to get there?"

I pointed at my grandfather's property on the map. "We just thought we'd fish over here. There ought to be a trout stream over here somewhere."

"You can't fish over there."

"Why not? Is it posted?"

"No, but it might just as well be. That property over there

belongs to a friend of MacKenzie's. MacKenzie is mighty touchy about people going over there. He especially don't like people from this camp going over there."

"I'm not afraid of any MacKenzie," I said.

Mrs. Fuller went back to her sweeping for a moment, then paused again. "There are other reasons you shouldn't go over there."

"What other reasons?"

"You'll find out if you try it."

"Well, I guess we'll try it."

"You'll be sorry," she said, as we went out the door.

George and I boldly stalked across Charlie Fuller's big common and plunged into the woods. The upper peninsula of Michigan was still a true wilderness in 1934 and it was no place for a couple of city boys like George and me. I know I'd never seen anything to compare with the forest I found myself in that morning. It had been fifty years since the last logs were cut in that area and I don't think anyone had set foot in it since. There were no paths and no landmarks. At first we started off on what we thought was the shortest route. Above us towered the second-growth pines. All about was tangled undergrowth. There were stumps and bushes and small trees growing so close together that it was difficult to push between them. Berry bushes reached out from everywhere to catch our clothes, scratch our faces and necks, and tear our hands. The fishing poles didn't help any. They snagged on something every other step we took. In the first full hour of struggling through this almost impenetrable tangle we covered about a quarter of a mile. It was then that George decided the going would be easier down at the water's edge. It was different, but it wasn't easier. We found ourselves in swampy ground that sucked at our shoes. Sometimes we sank in the muck up to our knees. Soon we began to come to streams. Inland these streams would have been innocent little brooks that could be forded or jumped. Down near the lake, where we were,

103

they were raging torrents, ten feet across and six feet deep. George was standing on the bank of one of them when the ground suddenly gave way under him and the next thing I knew he was in water over his head. I had to stick out my fishing pole and let him grab hold of it so I could pull him out. I tried to wade across the next stream we came to. I took only two steps and I was in water up to my chest. The water was icy. Finally, at a little after ten in the morning we had sense enough to go inland again. By then our clothes were torn and our faces and hands were scratched and bleeding and we were wet through. We fought on with determination and at a little before one o'clock we came out on a nose of high ground. From it we could look back at Charlie Fuller's camp three miles across the water. We flopped down on the ground and stretched out to rest. George shook his head in a discouraged manner.

"We couldn't live here, even if we found a place that looked good," he said. "How would we ever get into it and out of it?"

"There must be some way," I said. "Alec MacKenzie said we could use his boat."

"We'd have to row four or five miles across this lake and back just for a free place to pitch our tent. You're welcome to it. I'm going to stay in a free place that's easier to get to. That's Alec MacKenzie's camp." He climbed to his feet. "Come on! Let's get the hell out of here."

We turned around and started back, following the swathe we'd already made through the woods when we could, but we still had to put up with those berry bushes and all that undergrowth. It was well after six o'clock in the evening when we sank down on the bench of our picnic table, completely exhausted.

While I got out the cooking utensils, George moved around to build the smudges. It was about the time I squatted down to put the bacon on the fire that I began to itch. At first I thought it was the mosquitoes, but before long I was itching all over. George was itching, too, and he was really grumbling about the mosquitoes. He wasn't content to make just four fires for smudges. He was building them all over the place. About halfway through the meal I happened to glance at my wrists. They were swollen and covered with a rash. My ankles itched, too, so I rolled down my sox. My legs were covered with that same swollen redness and rash. George was much worse than I was. He had the swelling and the rash on his face and neck. The itching and the inflammation got worse by the minute. It was impossible to sit down so we just paced up and down in agony. It must have been after nine when our savior arrived. A young man, about our own age, dressed in overalls, came sauntering down the hill from the big house and walked into the circle of firelight. He didn't bother to introduce himself. He just glanced at us and then stepped quickly over to take a closer look at George.

"Jesus Christ!" he exclaimed. "You got it bad! Where were you? Over on the north shore of the lake?"

George nodded.

"Boy! I wish I'd seen you first. I could have told you not to go over there. Anybody around these parts could have. It's one great big, solid bed of poison ivy over there. They even had a big sign posted in the CC barracks warning people that it was off limits."

"Did Mrs. Fuller know that?" I asked him.

"Of course, she knew it."

"Why didn't she tell us?"

"Her? She wouldn't warn her best friend if he was about to step on a rattlesnake. You don't know old Charlie and his wife." He turned around and looked at me. "You got anything for it?"

"Nope," I said.

"You wait here just a minute," he said. "I'll be right back." He trotted off up the hill into the night. In about five minutes he was back with a big bottle of milky-looking liquid.

He shook it up and told us to hold out our hands. "Rub it on—all over," he said. "It might do you some good and then again it might not. I guess it depends on what kind of skin you've got. Anyway, it helps me."

I spread the lotion all over my body. It was cool and soothing and the itching began to stop. It didn't seem to help George at all, however. After a few minutes our benefactor pulled him over into the light again. He whistled.

"If I was you, I'd go over to Curtis the first thing in the morning," he said. "There's a doctor over there can fix you up with some other kind of stuff. He handles a lot of poison ivy cases because this whole area is full of it."

"Where's Curtis?" George asked.

"It's a little town over at the other end of the lake. Mostly Finns and Indians. It's about nine miles by road. Less than that across the lake."

"Nine miles?" George groaned.

"I know. Your car's broke down. You don't have to worry none, though. Once you get to MacKenzie's place, there's a lot of traffic. You can get a ride easy." He scratched his head and then held out his hand. "I'm Don Hopkins. I'm the hired man around here, but not for long. I'm getting out of here on Sunday night. I was in the CCs until my outfit moved up to Lake Superior. They're building some jetties up there and I can't take that cold water. I'm thinking of going down to the lower peninsula and joining up with a CC outfit I heard about down to Grayling. You know anything about the CC outfits down there?"

"Nope," I said. "You must like the CCs."

"They're not bad. I don't guess you'd like them, but for a fellow like me, they're just what the doctor ordered. Living's pretty hard around here."

"You come from around here?" I asked him.

"Yep. I was born in one of them cabins you passed comin' out here from Germfask and graduated from school up to Seney. I guess I know everybody within forty miles of here and some that don't come from here. My old man is a greenskeeper down to the Blaney golf course and my mother makes the beds at the Lodge." He reached across and took a brand from the fire and lit a cigarette. "You aren't from these parts?"

"Nope. Do you know Alec MacKenzie?"

"Sure. Knowed him all my life." He cocked his head and gave me a half smile. "I guess you'd be wanting to know about Jean. Everybody wants to know about Jean."

"Who's Jean?"

"That's MacKenzie's granddaughter. Mmmmmm, mmm-mmph. She is something."

"Yeah, I guess I've seen her. She's pretty good-looking."

"She's hot stuff, too. Take it from me. I know. Only trouble is, she's stuck up. She wouldn't even go out with our lieutenant in the CCs." He shook his head. "The only ones she goes out with are those rich snots who hang out down to Blaney Lodge."

"What's she got to be so stuck up about?" George said. "I don't see nothing around here that amounts to much."

Don Hopkins cast a peculiar glance at him, as though he didn't like the remark. "I guess you don't know much about the upper peninsula, do you?"

"Not much," George said.

"Well, it ain't as bad as you city fellows think it is."

"Don't get so huffy," George said. "I've only seen three houses between here and Germfask and they all look like the people were starving to death."

"One of them houses happened to belong to my old man," Don said. "I was born in one of them."

"Hey!" I said, "You two guys cut it out. What about this Jean MacKenzie dame, Don?" I was trying to change the subject as much as anything else, although I was curious about her.

"She's loaded. The whole MacKenzie family is loaded. Old Alec must own about half the upper peninsula. That place he's got over there in Germfask is just one of his houses. He's got a big mansion over to the Soo. A lot of people call him the governor of the upper peninsula. It ain't quite that bad. He's only the governor when the Democrats are in, which is right now. People say that he got old Albert Sleeper to build that road up to Curtis during the last time the Democrats was in power, just so he could get into his property. How do you think we got that CC battalion in here? I'll tell you why. Because old Alec wanted that road built across the swamp so he wouldn't have to drive thirty miles every time he wanted to go over to his camp. I heard tell a couple of months ago that the CCs was going to build a road from the Newberry highway down to the north shore of the lake when they get done with those jetties."

"Now, that's interesting," I said. "Very interesting."

"I don't put much stock in it. The Democrats got to get re-elected first and I don't think they got much chance since old Comstock closed the banks last year."

"What about this Jean?" George said. "Does she live over to the Soo?"

"Nope. She lives down to Chicago. Dave MacKenzie, that's Alec's son, married the daughter of one of those rich fellows from down at Blaney. He's a big-shot doctor down in Chicago. Jean's studying to be a doctor herself at one of those universities down there, but she comes up here every summer to stay with old Alec. Been coming ever since I can remember. She don't have much to do with us natives, though. All she does is play golf and tennis and swim down at the Lodge. She's got a horse over at Alec's camp and every afternoon she goes over there and rides him around." He raised his eyebrows. "I'll tell you something else about her if you promise not to tell anybody."

"What's that?"

"She goes swimming bare ass every morning at a cove over to Alec's place. Brrrrrr." He shook himself. "Just thinking about it gives me the heebie jeebies."

"How do you know she goes swimming bare ass?" George said.

"Because I seen her. I see her every morning. I make it a point to see her."

"I'll bet the CC boys enjoy *that*," I said.

"Naw. I didn't discover it until after the outfit moved up to Superior. Me and some of the other CCs stole one of Charlie's boats last summer. He charges about three times what a boat is worth and none of the CCs could afford it. So we came over here one night and took it. We repainted it and hid it in some bushes over in the cove. About a month ago I went over to see if it was still there and while I was nosing around in the bushes, Jean comes out of the woods. The first thing I know she strips off her bathing suit and jumps in the water. She come right across the cove to where I was and climbed out on the bank. She was so close to me I could have reached out and grabbed her by the boobs. Well, naturally, if that kind of thing is going on every morning, I might just as well take advantage of it. What I mean, she's built like a brick shit house. I'd sure like to have a little of that. Makes me squirm just to think about it." He threw his cigarette in the fire. "You know what? You fellows ought to have that boat. The CCs aren't here any more and I'm leaving on Sunday. It could save you paying old Charlie Shyster every time you want to go fishing."

"We're not planning to stay around here very long, either," I said. "We're going over to MacKenzie's camp and stay."

"Old Alec ain't exactly what I'd call generous. He'll squeeze everything out of you he can get. You'd better let me show you that boat. It will save you money."

"I don't think we'll need it. Alec promised to let us have a boat free."

"He did?" Don scratched his head. "That ain't like him. I ain't never heard of him givin' anything away before. You must have something he wants."

"Yeah, I guess maybe we do, but I think the main reason is that he and my grandfather were good friends back in the old days."

"Yeah? You better not tell old Charlie you're a friend of MacKenzie's. He'd run you right out of here with a shotgun. Those two been fightin' for twenty years or more. That's the reason old Alec wanted that road built across the swamp, if you ask me. Just to spite Charlie." He straightened up out of his squat and looked over his shoulder. "Oh-oh, here comes Charlie now. Don't forget to keep your mouth shut about what I told you."

Charlie Fuller came striding into the firelight. He looked around at us.

"Mosquitoes pretty bad tonight, boys?"

"You can't breathe without inhaling a few of them," Don said. "This ain't much of a place to camp. I sure wouldn't want to stay down here."

"You just keep your good-for-nothing opinions to yourself," Charlie said. "If I want them, I'll ask for them. Now you run on up and open up Cabin Eight. I just had a phone call from town. Some folks will be out here in half an hour."

"Okay," Don said, and walked off into the night.

"You boys don't worry none about these mosquitoes," Charlie said. "You'll get used to them after a while and the mosquitoes will get used to you. Then they'll go off some place lookin' for new blood." He seemed to think this was a good joke for he laughed. Then he sobered and looked at me and stepped over to look closer. "Yeah, I heard you went over on the north shore this morning. Too bad! You good-for-nothing city kids won't listen to nobody, will you?"

"We'd listen if anybody told us anything," I said.

"My wife told you you'd be sorry. That ought to be enough for anybody with a brain the size of a pea. You got to have everything spelled out for you?"

He turned and walked off toward the big house.

"He *is* a son of a bitch, isn't he?" George said.

NINE

That was a very bad night. The ointment helped me, but poor George was in agony. He didn't sleep a wink. He paced up and down in the firelight scratching himself until he began to bleed. When it got daylight I felt so sorry for him that I just took the ten-dollar bill out of my pocket and told him to get started for Curtis to see the doctor. He didn't even wait for breakfast. After he'd trudged off down the road, I cooked the usual bacon, washed up, and then went looking for Don Hopkins. I found him wrestling a milk can into the back door of the big house.

"I thought I'd take you up on that boat," I said. "George has gone over to Curtis to see the doctor and I figured he might enjoy a nice mess of fish when he comes back."

"Soon's I get this milk up to the kitchen and get the fires built up, I'll be takin' the cows out to pasture," he said. He pointed out toward the barn. "You go down there where the spring is. You'll find a trail that leads up over the hill through the woods. On the other side of that hill is a big stump. You wait for me there and I'll take you where the boat is. Just make sure you don't let old Charlie see you, though. If he saw us going off somewhere together, it would be just like him to follow us. He don't trust nobody, especially guys like you and me. I'll be along in about twenty minutes."

"I'll just pretend I'm looking around the camp."

I didn't have to pretend at all. Up until that moment I hadn't seen anything. I began by wandering over to the edge of the bluff to look out over the lake. There was a long flight of stairs that led down to the dock and I could see five or six people out there putting gear in boats. I went down the steps and strolled out on the pier and looked at a couple of the boats and then turned around to go back up to the common. Right at the end of the dock, on the shore, was a boathouse and the door was standing open so I went over and looked in. There was a long glass showcase on one side of the room. It was filled with various kinds of fishing tackle. At the back was a rack which contained twenty or thirty outboard motors. To the right there was a long wooden counter and on it was something that immediately took my eye. It seemed absolutely incongruous in a place run by a man like Charlie Fuller. I was looking at a slot machine—a one-armed bandit. I went in and stood before it, staring at it. After some moments I fished around in my pocket and pulled out a nickel and reached up and put it in the slot. I was just reaching for the lever when someone came up behind me. I turned to see Charlie. He was looking at me very suspiciously.

"You want to rent a boat? If you're fixing to go fishing, I'll tell you right now, I get a dollar an hour for my boats. If you want an outboard motor, that's an extra two dollars an hour."

"Mr. Fuller, I couldn't afford to rent one of your oars. I was just looking around to see what you have here."

"I don't like people snooping around. I got better things to do than follow the likes of you around. Come on! Get out of here. If you're not going to buy anything I want to lock this place up."

"Wait until I play my nickel off on this slot machine."

"Hurry it up!" he snapped.

I pulled the lever and the wheels began to spin. First one cherry dropped into place, then another, then a bell. There was a click and four nickels fell into the little bowl at the bottom of the machine. I scooped them out, put them in my pocket, and started for the door.

"Hey!" Charlie bellowed, as though in great pain. "Ain't you going to take those cherries off there?"

I was well aware that it was considered unethical to go off and leave a winning combination showing on a slot machine, but I was fed up with Charlie and I thought he needed a lesson.

"You said to hurry it up," I said, "and I'm hurrying it up."

I bounced up the stairs two steps at a time and reached the bluff. Just as I passed out of hearing I heard the sound of the lever being pulled as Charlie got the cherries off. I wasted no time in getting to the barn and following the trail over the hill into the woods. It was some minutes before Don Hopkins came along, driving the cows ahead of him.

"What did you do to make Charlie so mad?" he asked me as I got up from the stump. "He came into the barn a few minutes ago fit to be tied."

I told him about the slot machine.

"You must be the only fellow who ever made any money out of that machine," he said. "He's got it set so that it pays off about four nickels for every fifty you put in. Not only that, he takes a lot of the money out of the jackpot box. On most nickel machines you stand to take in three to four dollars out of a jackpot, but on Charlie's you're lucky to get a dollar and a half out of it. Some of the CCs got so mad at that machine last summer that they were going to throw it in the lake. They would have, too, if Charlie hadn't hid it. If I was you, I wouldn't play it no more."

We followed the cows along the path for a quarter of a

mile or more and came to a clearing. Don shooed the cows into it and then beckoned for me to follow him. The path re-entered a thick woods and climbed another hill. When we came over the top of it I found myself looking down through the trees at a little cove that stretched across for perhaps seventy-five yards. Don stopped and looked around carefully and then led the way down the slope to the water's edge. Here there was an enormous, thick clump of some kind of reeds or bushes. Don put his finger up to his lips and motioned for me to stay where I was, then he got down on his hands and knees, parted the bushes and crawled in. I couldn't see him, but in a moment he popped up. He was not more than ten feet from me. Grinning, he signaled for me to do the same as he had and when I got down on my hands and knees I found him holding the bushes apart for me. I crawled along after him for a few feet until he motioned for me to sit down.

"You can't see into these bushes for more than two or three feet," he said, "so don't worry. Just keep absolutely quiet." He pointed off across the cove. I could see the other shore quite plainly if I ducked low enough.

We sat there for ten minutes, whispering back and forth, and then he nudged me and pointed. Across the water I could see some kind of movement in the undergrowth and then, suddenly, Jean MacKenzie burst into view. She was wearing that black, one-piece bathing suit and carrying a white towel. She went quickly to a tree and hung the towel on a limb and then, without bothering to even look around, she slipped the straps of the suit off her shoulders and let the whole business slide to the ground. She stood there for a moment on tiptoe, absolutely nude, and then she took one or two quick steps and dove gracefully into the water. She swam straight toward us with long, graceful strokes and finally climbed out on shore about twenty-five feet away. She stood there for only a moment or two, tucking her hair under her bathing cap. Then she turned and dove into

114

the water and swam back across the cove. When she
climbed out on the other side she ran quickly to the tree and
took down the towel and rubbed herself vigorously. For
just a moment after she finished toweling, she stood there
looking around, then she took off her bathing cap and her
hair fell down to her waist. It was dark red hair—auburn
colored—and for just a moment as she stood there I thought
of all those artists' paintings I'd seen of Eve in the Garden
of Eden. Quickly she swooped the hair up, twisted it two or
three times around her head and fastened it in some way.
Then she grabbed up the bathing suit and slipped into it
and drew it on. Within fifteen minutes of the time she arrived at the cove she had disappeared back into the woods.

"She sure is something, ain't she?" Don said.

"She's beautiful."

"She's built, too."

"Is that all there is to it?"

"What more do you want? Come on, let's go take a look
at the boat." We crawled through the bushes for another
thirty feet and there was a rowboat tucked away. "This
here boat's in good shape," Don said. "The CC boys calked
it this spring. There's one thing you have to remember about
using it. Be sure you stay down in this part of the lake. Charlie never comes over here because it's too close to MacKenzie's. Just remember, if he ever sees you in this boat, he'll
take it away from you. After all, it was his in the first place."

I promised to be careful and we climbed out of the bushes
and started back toward the camp.

"I can't get over that girl," I said. "Boy, I'd sure like to
get to know her."

"You ought not have any trouble," he said. "With your
grandfather being a friend of her grandfather it ought to
be easy."

"Naw! I met her the other day when George and I
stopped over to Alec MacKenzie's house in Germfask. I
don't think she even knows who I am."

"Oh, well, if you really want to get some place with her, I could probably fix you up good."

"How?"

"I've knowed her ever since she started coming up here. Sometimes, when there ain't any of her little boy friends around, she's nice to me. Anyway, tonight's Saturday night and I usually pick up an extra dollar or two by waiting table at the dances down to the Lodge. She's always there on Saturday night, getting juiced up. I'll tell her all about you. I'll butter it up good. I know what she goes for and I'll have her wantin' to meet you."

After I left Don, I went over to my tent and got out my fishing pole and then dug some worms and put them in a can. Keeping one eye out for Charlie Fuller, I went back over to the cove and shoved the boat out into the water. I rowed off toward Alec MacKenzie's camp and shipped the oars and baited my hook. I sat in that rowboat for six hours and I never got so much as a nibble. It was almost three o'clock in the afternoon when I finally gave up and put the rowboat back in its hiding place. I was quite dejected as I trudged back to the camp. When I came to the icehouse, Don Hopkins stuck his head out the door.

"Hey! What have you got in that can?"

"Worms," I said.

"What for?"

"Bait."

"Boy, you don't know anything at all, do you? These fish up here in the upper peninsula are cannibals. The only thing they eat are other fish. You got to have minnows." He held up a small pail for me to see. "I'll fill this up with minnows before I go tonight and I'll leave it right here beside the door. Use them when you go out fishing tomorrow and you'll catch something."

When I got back to the tent I found George busy washing out some clothes. He seemed to be feeling very chipper.

"That doctor fixed me up good," he said, holding out his

arms for me to see. They were painted with some kind of purple ointment. "All I have to do is keep spreading this stuff on for a day or two."

"I'm glad *you* feel better," I said, "because now I'm not feeling so hot. I've been out fishing all day and I didn't get so much as a nibble. At this rate we can starve to death before long. I guess it's more bacon for supper."

"Cheer up," George said. "I brought you back a surprise from Curtis." He went over to the car and rummaged around in the food box we kept in the back. When he turned around he was holding up two big, beautiful sirloin steaks. "Curtis is a lot better town than Germfask. They even have a butcher over there."

I must admit that it took me a few minutes to get the real significance of those steaks. I was happy to see them. They came into my view at the very moment when I was getting tired of our incessant diet of bacon. Yet, the minute I saw them, red lights began flashing in my mind. It eventually came to me.

"George, how much did those steaks cost you?"

"I don't know. I guess it must have been about two dollars. You see, I got some other things along with them. I bought some more bread and some ears of corn and some more bacon and a dozen eggs. The whole thing came to about four dollars so I guess the steaks must have been about a dollar apiece."

"George," I said quietly, "how much change have you got from that ten bucks?"

He actually seemed surprised. "Well, none. The doctor charged me four bucks and the ointment cost me two dollars and, like I said, the food cost me four dollars."

I got up from where I was sitting. I don't think I've ever been as mad at anyone in my whole life. "Goddamn you, George," I exploded. "This is Saturday afternoon. We left home a week ago tomorrow morning. We're now down to ten dollars and eleven cents. Just what the hell do you think we're going to live on for the rest of the summer?"

"Oh, for Christ's sake—," he said.

"Don't you 'for Christ's sake' me, you horse's ass," I said. "I've had enough of you. You know what our situation is, and then you go right ahead and spend that money. I don't ever want to see you again or have anything more to do with you."

"But—" He actually looked distressed.

"Stick it up your ass," I said, and turned on my heel and walked away. I must admit that I didn't know what to do at that moment. I just wanted to get away from him and sit down and think. I do know that I was convinced that there wasn't any use of going any further with this whole business. I stumbled along the road that led down the hill from Charlie Fuller's place and eventually came to the place where the road to MacKenzie's camp led off across the swamp. I sat down on a rock there and tried to decide on a course of action. I'd almost made up my mind to go back up to the camp and pack up my stuff and start hitchhiking home when I saw a car come bouncing toward me across the CCC road. It came to the corner and skidded around the turn to head for Germfask. It was that same little Ford roadster and it was driven by Jean MacKenzie. I watched the taillights disappear in the gathering dusk.

"Well," I said to myself, "there's no use in starting out tonight. I might just as well enjoy myself while I'm here. Tomorrow morning, after the exhibition, I'll make up my mind what I'm going to do."

I strolled slowly back to the camp. It was well after dark when I got there. George had left his dirty plate on the table after finishing his dinner. I noticed that he had gotten his suitcase out of the car and had put on his good clothes while I was gone. It suddenly struck me that he might have made up his mind to do the same thing I'd decided to do. It was several minutes before he came strolling down the hill from the big house. He was, indeed, all dressed up and

118

he seemed to be quite nonchalant, as though nothing at all had happened.

"What are you all dressed up for?" I asked.

"I'm going over to Curtis."

"You just came back from Curtis."

"They have a dance over there every Saturday night."

"Who are you going to dance with? The butcher?"

"Aw, lay off, will you? I'm sorry I spent your money. Why don't you let well enough alone? You ought to get it off your mind and come on over to Curtis with me. It would cheer you up. There are a lot of girls over there. I met one in the doctor's office and she invited me to come back. I'm pretty sure I could get you a date."

"That's all I need. Until we get some more money, I don't even want to think about any dates."

"Have it your own way," he said. "I'm not going to sit here and wait for the world to come to an end." With that he just turned and walked off into the night. He didn't even pick up his dirty plate from the table.

That was a lonely Saturday night. I think everyone in Charlie Fuller's camp went off to enjoy themselves somewhere. I dug my steak and ears of corn out of the food box and cooked them and ate them, then washed up the dishes, and went to bed in a cloud of mosquitoes. When I woke up the next morning, George hadn't come home. I didn't wait for him. I cooked up some bacon for breakfast, got out my fishing rod, and started for the cove. On the way I picked up the pail of minnows Don had left for me. I stashed everything away in the boat and then crawled through the bushes and sat down. I must have waited a half hour before Jean MacKenzie appeared. Her performance was exactly the same as it had been on the previous morning. It was a fine show while it lasted and at the end of it, I'm afraid, I'd given up any thoughts of going home.

After Jean had gone, I went over and got in the boat and rowed out into the lake. This time I got a bite right away.

I'd never caught a real fighting fish before and I had a hard time landing that one. There were moments when my light fishing rod was bent almost double. When I got it into the boat I found it to be a fine, big northern pike, a little over two feet long. It whetted my appetite for more sport and I rebaited my hook and cast again. I didn't catch my second fish until after ten o'clock, but it was almost as big as the first one and it put up a tremendous fight. After that second one I didn't get any more bites. I rowed around, changing position, three or four more times and finally gave it up, but I was more than satisfied. At that moment, the whole situation seemed immeasurably improved to me. At last we were catching fish. At last we were living off the land. Things couldn't help but be better.

When I came back to the tent that afternoon, George was there, spreading more ointment over his body.

"Where were you all night?" I asked him.

"In Curtis. That girl is really hot stuff. We sat on a park bench in front of the dance hall until daylight this morning. I think I'm going to get some place with her."

"You're not going to get anyplace with a girl on a park bench in front of a dance hall. Any idiot knows that."

"You don't know Curtis and you don't know Finns. That's some town and those Finns are some girls."

"I always heard those Finn men were pretty tough. You'd better be careful monkeying around with their girls." I held up the fish for him to see. "Look what I got for supper. How about giving me a hand cleaning them?"

"I haven't got time," he said. "I'm just on my way back to Curtis. I have another date at six o'clock."

"Why didn't you just stay over there?"

"I forgot to take my poison ivy dope with me or I would have."

He didn't waste any time getting out of there. He'd cooked up some bacon for lunch and he'd just left his plate and the frying pan sitting on the table so I had to clean up his mess. Then I had to go to work on the fish. Cleaning fish was one of the things I'd sort of depended on George to do. It wasn't that I wanted him to do the dirty work. I just didn't know anything about cleaning fish. I knew they had to be scaled and I knew the insides had to be taken out of them and the heads cut off, but I'd never tried it before. I did my best, but long before I was done, I'd lost all taste for the job and for the fish. It was dark before I put them on the fire to cook. When I ate them, I didn't like them. If I hadn't been good and hungry, I don't think I could have eaten them. With every minute that went by I was getting sicker of Germfask, the upper peninsula, and everything to do with them. I'd just finished cleaning up after supper when Don Hopkins delivered the final blow. He came walking into the firelight from up at the big house. He was all dressed up and carrying a suitcase.

"I'm on my way," he said. "Wish me luck."

"Where are you going?"

"Down to Grayling, like I said. I'm going to join a CC outfit down there that's planting trees. Do me a favor, will you? Don't tell old Charlie I've gone. I want to be a long ways away before he discovers it."

"What's the matter? You stealing something?"

"Shucks, no. He'd try to argue me out of it. He'd probably even go over to Blaney and try to talk to my folks. Say, speaking of Blaney, I fixed you up good with Jean MacKenzie. I fixed you up real good."

"How?"

"I told her there was a rich college kid staying over here, big athlete with a great big shiny car. Boy, did she fall for it! Asked me all kinds of questions."

"What did you tell her all that stuff for? She'd never fall for that stuff if she knew the truth. Wait until she sees that big shiny car." I waved my hand at the old Buick.

"That's the kind of stuff she goes for. I know. You don't have to worry about her ever seein' that old car. She won't ever come over here to Charlie's place. Old Alec would skin her alive. As far as the rest of it goes, all you have to do is act rich. She's all set up for you. She made me promise to introduce you when you come down to the dance at Blaney next Saturday night."

"That's nice, but how are you going to work that? You're going down to Grayling."

"That won't make any difference. All you have to do is go down to Blaney Lodge next Saturday night and when you see her you go over and tell her that Don Hopkins was telling you about her. She'll know who you are."

"How am I going to get into a dance at Blaney?"

"You don't have to worry none about that. You just ask old Charlie for a card. He and all the other fishing camps around here have reciprocal arrangements with the Lodge. He lets the people at Blaney Lodge fish out of his camp and they let his guests go to the dances and use the golf course."

"I know, but I only pay a dollar and a half a week here. Charlie even makes me use the outhouse. He'll never give me a pass to go to Blaney."

"That don't make no difference. You're a guest and it says right up there in the big house what all the guests are entitled to. You tell old Charlie to come across or you'll sue him." He shifted his feet uneasily. "Speaking of suing somebody, I hate to ask you for it, but I wonder if I could have that two dollars now."

"What two dollars?"

"The two bucks George borrowed from me."

"When did he borrow two bucks from you?"

"He borrowed a buck last night and he borrowed another buck this afternoon. He said if I had to leave before he got around to paying it back that you'd give it to me. I'll need it when I get down to Grayling."

I shook my head. I was so mad I couldn't talk. I just squatted there staring into the fire for about five minutes and then I pulled my money out of my pocket and peeled off two ones and gave them to him. He thanked me, shook hands, and walked off into the night. I didn't move for a good half hour, then I got up and went over to the car, and began pulling my things out. I put everything I could into a pack that I carried on my back. The rest I made into a bundle and tied it securely with a rope so that I could carry it. After I had everything ready, I went over to the picnic table and wrote a note to George.

TEN

If I'd been anywhere else but Manistique Lake, I'm afraid the trip and my long friendship with George French would have ended then and there. Unfortunately, there was just no way to get out of the place. I carried my pack and my bundle down to the corner below Charlie Fuller's place. They were too heavy and too bulky to carry any farther so I sat down on the rock and waited for a car to come along and give me a ride. I was still sitting there at daylight the next morning when George came plodding across the road that the CCC had built.

"What are you doing there?" he asked me.

"I'm on my way home, George."

"What? The least you could have done was tell me about it."

"I left you a note on the picnic table."

"And you were going to walk out just like that and leave me all alone up here?"

"You won't be alone. You've got a girl over in Curtis."

"But I don't have any money. What kind of a prick are you anyway?"

"I'm just getting out of here while I've still got enough

to pay my way across on the ferry at St. Ignace. I don't care how you manage it. Why don't you borrow some money? You're pretty good at that. I'm sure somebody else will pay it back for you."

He rubbed his hand over his face. "So that's what you're sore about?"

"You're damned right I'm sore. What did you think I was going to be?"

"But you never give me a chance to explain. You always get in a big huff and walk off. I could have told you about those two dollars I borrowed. But you weren't around when I wanted to. Anyway, I knew you'd be sore and that there wasn't any use in trying to tell you when you're like that."

"George, it's not just the two dollars. That's bad enough. It's the whole thing that's been going on around here. It's the ten dollars you blew on Saturday. It's the hamburgers you always want for lunch and the apple pie à la mode when you know we're hard up. It's the driving seventy miles out of our way just to see a girl. It's the whole goddamned business and I'm fed up with it."

"If you'd let me tell you about the ten dollars, I could explain it."

"All right. Explain it."

"Well, before we came up here, my mother told me to write her a letter if I got in trouble—real trouble—and she'd send me some money. She don't have much, but she guessed she could spare a little. When I got that poison ivy all over me, I figured I was in real trouble so when I was over in Curtis Saturday I wrote her a letter and asked for twenty dollars. She'll send it to me, you wait and see. It will be here in two or three days and I'll pay you back the money you gave me."

"It's not good enough, George. Even if you get twenty bucks, which I doubt, I've had enough of this crap. I'm going home."

"But you can't do that. Not yet!"

"Why not? What's there to stay around here for? I've seen the property. I've done what I really came up here to do and, I can tell you, it's a lot more expensive living up here than it is at home."

"Well, what about the car?"

"What about it?"

"We can't go off and just leave it sitting there. I want that car. It's mine. I earned it by driving you up here in it."

He really wanted that car and he wanted me to stay there until we got it fixed and could get it back home. He sat there on that rock and he argued with me. He pleaded with me. I don't know how long he argued, but I do know we sat there long enough to see Jean MacKenzie come skidding around the corner on her way for her morning dip and we were still there when she went back the other way after her morning dip.

"All right," I said finally. "I'll stay one more week. If we don't get the ring gear at the end of the week and if we don't get the car fixed, that's just too bad. I'm going home no matter what."

He heaved a sigh of relief. "Thanks," he said.

"There's a couple of other things," I said. "You're going to have to do a couple of things around that camp besides build smudges. You're going to have to wash your dishes, for instance. You're going to have to help clean the fish."

"All right," he said. "I'll do it. What do you want me to do first?"

"Go catch us a mess of fish for supper."

He picked up my bundle and helped me carry it back up to the tent and we put the stuff away. I cooked up some bacon and eggs for breakfast and he even washed the dishes. After that I led him over to the cove and showed him the boat and the minnows and got him all ready to go, giving him the instructions that Don had given me about staying down in MacKenzie's corner of the lake.

"What are you going to do?" he asked me, just before he pushed off.

"I'm going to walk into Germfask and see if we've got any answers to those letters we sent out. That ring gear might just possibly be there. Anyway, even if it isn't, I'm going to talk to Alec MacKenzie and see if I can find a way to move this car over to his place."

There was no mail, and when I went to MacKenzie's store I got some bad news. MacKenzie wouldn't be back from Lansing until the end of the week. That meant we'd have to spend another dollar and a half and stay at Fuller's camp a second week. There was only one good thing about that whole trip into town. By some miracle, I got a ride both ways. It was only a little after two o'clock when I came walking back into the camp. I looked around for George and soon discovered that he had not yet returned from fishing. I decided to cook up a little more bacon and have a sandwich for lunch.

We'd been keeping all our food in a small cardboard box on the floor in the back of the car and I walked over to get out the bacon. I knew where the box was and I knew that the bacon was lying on the top of the pile of food. I simply didn't pay much attention to what I was doing. I just reached my arm over the back door and grabbed at the bacon. I suddenly felt as if someone had shot ten thousand volts of electricity in my hand. I fell backward and then cautiously looked over the back of the front seat. There was an animal sitting in our food box, staring maliciously up at me out of his little pig eyes. He'd been finishing off the bacon. I'd never seen one before in my life, but I knew at once that I was looking at a porcupine. He was an angry porcupine, too. Never having seen a porcupine before, I didn't know how to deal with one, but I wasn't exactly interested in getting rid of him at the moment. The only thing I could think about was how badly my hand hurt. It was awful. I looked down at it and I could see three little quills sticking out of the back of it. I reached down with my other hand, intending to pull them out. I discovered that just touching one of them was worse than getting them in there in the first place. The pain was so excruciating that I had to hang onto the side of the car. I didn't know what to do, but in desperation it occurred to me that someone up at the big house might have some experience with this kind of thing. Hurriedly, holding my injured hand carefully in the other one so as not to jar it, I walked up the hill. Charlie Fuller was standing behind the counter of his store, talking to a customer. I held out my hand for him to see. I should have known better than to expect any sympathy from Charlie.

"Porcupine quills," he sneered. "Even my old dog knows enough not to monkey around with a porcupine."

"I know, but what do I do?" I asked.

"Ain't nothing to do but get those quills out of there," he said. He walked around the end of the counter and disappeared into the kitchen. He was back in a moment, carrying a pair of pliers. "This is going to hurt," he said.

That was the understatement of all time. Just touching one of those quills tenderly was enough to make me dizzy, but Charlie wasn't in the least gentle. He just grabbed one brusquely with the pliers and pulled and it came out. Things started going around and the next thing I knew I was sitting on the floor with my back against the counter. The customer had been standing there observing all this and he now held up his hand.

"Before you take another of those out," he told Charlie, "we'd better give him something. I'll be right back." He turned and trotted over to the stairs and went up them. When he came back down he was carrying a water glass with an inch or two of amber fluid in it. He thrust it at me. "Drink this," he said. I smelled it. It was whiskey. I threw back my head and gulped it down and I felt better right away. I held out my hand to Charlie. He didn't take it. He was glaring at the customer.

"Jackson," he said, "that was whiskey."

"Of course, it was whiskey," Mr. Jackson said.

"My wife and I don't allow any whiskey on these premises," Charlie said. "We got three young girls to bring up."

"Oh, for Christ's sake, Charlie," Mr. Jackson said, "stop your arguing and get those quills out of there before it wears off."

Charlie continued to glare at him for another moment or two and then he reached out roughly and grabbed my hand. He very nearly killed me, but he grabbed the quills with his pliers, one after the other, and pulled them out. All I could do was sit there. I couldn't move. I couldn't talk. I couldn't see. Mr. Jackson knelt down and watched me.

"Are you all right?" he asked me.

"I guess I'll make it," I said. "Give me a few minutes."

He picked up the hand and looked at it. "I guess I'd better get something for this," he said. "I'll be right back."

"No more whiskey," Charlie said, as Mr. Jackson started for the stairs.

When Mr. Jackson came back he had some iodine and some bandage. He put the iodine on the back of my hand and wrapped a bandage around it. He made me stay there leaning on the counter for ten minutes before he'd let me get up off the floor. Even then, he walked with me all the way down to my tent to make sure I got there. Charlie didn't say a word, of course, or pay any attention to me.

It took me all the rest of the afternoon to get over those porcupine quills. The hand hurt terribly and I was literally so weak that I didn't feel like doing anything but sitting there on the picnic bench. (The porcupine had disappeared with the last of the bacon.) When George came in from his fishing about five o'clock, he held up three fine pike. He cleaned them and cooked them and we ate them. It was about an hour after supper when Charlie came striding down the hill in the dark to stand by our fire.

"Either one of you seen that good-for-nothing Don?" he asked us.

"Nope. Not all day," I said.

"He's cleared out, bag and baggage. He didn't even have the decency to tell me he was going." He peered from one to the other of us. "You boys planning to stay here another week?"

"I suppose you want another dollar and a half?"

"If you're going to stay another week, I'll be wanting another dollar and a half, but that ain't why I asked. I'll be needing another hired man to take Don's place and I just don't have time to run around the countryside looking for one. If either one of you boys wants the job, you can have it."

"How much do you pay, Mr. Fuller?"

"Three dollars and a half a week and room and board. If you work for me you get to sleep up to the house and take your meals with the family."

"That's not very much money," I said.

"That's quite a lot of money. You fellows are husky boys and you'd eat a lot. Anyway, it's enough to pay for your camping down here with something left over."

"Mr. Fuller, do you mean to tell me that we'd still have to pay for this camping ground, even if we worked for you?"

"Ain't but one of you going to be working for me. The other one's still going to be living down here. The tent will still be here. The car will still be here taking up my valuable ground. You ought to pay."

"No, thank you, Mr. Fuller. You can keep your job."

"Now, you wait a minute," George put in, glaring at me. "You might not want that job, but what makes you think I don't want it? I can use that three dollars and a half a week after what I've been through."

"Get your clothes, boy, and come up to the house and

I'll show you where you'll sleep. At least you'll be out of the mosquitoes." He turned to me. "While I'm down here, I might just as well collect the dollar and a half you owe me."

"Mr. Fuller, I don't owe you any dollar and a half. I'm paid up until Wednesday noon. That's when the week started. How do I know? I might get this car fixed and get out of here by then."

"If you're thinkin' of that, you'd better get it fixed by ten in the morning. *That's* when your week starts and I'll tell you right now I ain't going to give you one minute overtime."

He stuck out his chin and turned and stalked off. George hurried around picking up his belongings and then came over to say good-by.

"I'm ashamed of you, George," I said.

"Why?"

"For giving in like that."

"When Saturday comes around and I want to go to Curtis, I don't want to come around and get down on my hands and knees to you. You're as bad as he is."

"You're going to be sorry," I said.

I wasn't far wrong. I was lonesome, but I wasn't as bad off as Geroge was. I didn't even see him until just as I was going to bed the next night. That's when he came dragging down to the tent.

"Boy, am I pooped," he said.

"What have you been doing all day?"

"I started out this morning by milking twenty cows before breakfast. Then I had to carry three cans of milk up to the house, and take the cows out to pasture. After breakfast I sawed wood at the sawmill and carried ice to all the cabins. Then I got in a boat with Charlie and we went all the way up to the other end of the lake and seined for minnows. After that I had to get down on my hands and knees and

132

scrub out three cabins. That only took me to noon. I can't even remember what I did after noon. What time is it?"

"It's almost ten o'clock," I said.

"I can't even go to bed yet," he whined. "Charlie says there might be some more tourists about eleven o'clock. If they come I have to go and open up the cabins and put ice in the refrigerators for them and carry wood for the stoves."

The next night, on Wednesday, George came dragging down to the tent again.

"What day is it?" he said.

"Wednesday."

He groaned.

"Only Wednesday. I'll never make it to Saturday."

I didn't see him at all on Thursday. He went down to his room after supper and dropped off to sleep and didn't wake up until morning. By Friday afternoon I was worried enough about him to go looking for him. That's the way it was when you worked for Charlie.

ELEVEN

George went to work for Charlie Fuller on Monday, July 29, 1934. The next morning—a Tuesday—left by myself, I fell into a regular routine. It was not a complicated routine, but it was something like the way I had imagined life would be in the upper peninsula when I first started out on this journey. Perhaps the salient feature of it was that I didn't spend any money.

The first section of this routine involved the morning free show. I was up at a little after daylight, and after a quick cup of coffee and piece of toast—the porcupine had effectively removed the bacon from my diet—I grabbed up my fishing pole and the pail of minnows and headed for the cove. Jean MacKenzie arrived at her usual time and did her usual thing. After she had gone off and left me forlorn, I got in the boat and went after the day's food. I soon discovered that my hand was so sore from the porcupine quills that I couldn't row the boat well. Luckily, I caught two small pike within an hour from the time I started out and I decided to call it quits for the day.

I got back to the tent around nine o'clock and because I had absolutely nothing else to do, I decided to walk into

Germfask and see if our ring gear had come yet. I fully expected to walk both ways, but the prospect no longer frightened me.

I had gone about a mile that morning when a big, brand-new LaSalle sports coupé pulled up beside me. Driving it was Mr. Jackson, the man who had given me the whiskey and bandaged my hand the day before.

"How's the hand?" he asked me.

"It's pretty sore," I said, "but I guess I'll live."

"I'm taking some films over to the drugstore in Newberry to be developed," he said. "Do you want to ride along?"

I hadn't seen Newberry yet. "Sure," I said.

Mr. Jackson came from Battle Creek, it turned out. He was in the breakfast food business and obviously quite well off. We talked about several things on the way to Newberry, but mostly about that car. It was so new that it smelled new. In 1934, a LaSalle was considered to be a pretty fine car and in my own little Depression world I'd never known anyone with enough money to buy a new one. I must have impressed Mr. Jackson with my enthusiasm for it. After he'd finished his business in Newberry, he came back to the car and casually asked me if I'd like to do the driving on the way home. I wasn't going to miss a chance like that. As we approached Germfask, I suddenly remembered the ring gear and I asked him if he minded if I stopped at the post office to see if there was any mail. He told me to go ahead so I glided to a stop in front of the little box of a building. Just as I was getting out the door on the driver's side, that Ford roadster of Jean MacKenzie's came skidding around the corner of Alec's hotel building and slid to a stop nose-on with the LaSalle. I could see her looking at that pretty car as she got out to go into the post office and I knew that she was mightily impressed with it. I decided that the time had arrived to make my move.

"Hi!" I said to her as we met in the doorway. "Aren't you Jean MacKenzie?"

"I am," she said, giving me a big smile.

"We have a mutual friend, Don Hopkins."

"Oh, you're the fellow he was talking about." I saw her take another quick look at the LaSalle.

"He told me you'd be glad to show me around at Blaney Lodge."

"Why, I'd be very happy to," she said. "There's an awful nice bunch of kids down there. You say when."

"In a day or two," I said. "I'll get in touch with you."

I went back and climbed into the LaSalle and drove off. She waved her hand at me as I pulled away and I could see her in the rear-vision mirror looking after me. I felt like patting that LaSalle all the rest of the way out to Charlie's camp. Of course, after I got out to the camp and came down to earth while I was cleaning my fish, I began to have some readjustments in my thinking about Jean MacKenzie. I think I agreed with everything that George and Don Hopkins said she was. She was pretty dumb to fall for a line like that one Don had given her and she was probably a heartless snob on top of it all. The thing was that even without a heart and a mind, she still had a pretty good body and at the moment that was what interested me most. I was certainly not disgusted enough with her shortcomings to miss the daily spectacle the next morning.

My routine was interrupted slightly that Wednesday morning because I'd just nicely started to fish when I recalled that Charlie had warned me not to be late with my rent money. I had to row back to shore and go all the way up to the house. Mrs. Fuller was in the store when I got there and I decided to get even with her for not warning us about the poison ivy. I took up a whole hour of her valuable time making her write me out an elaborate receipt for that dollar and a half. I made her put down words and cross them out and finally came up with a document that read about as follows:

"Whereas I, Martha Fuller, spouse of Charles Fuller,

owner of Fuller's Camp, Germfask, Luce County, State of Michigan, have received this day and date from Edmund G. Love of Flint, Genesee County, State of Michigan, the sum of one dollar and fifty cents ($1.50), in payment of rent for camping space in the lower area of this aforesaid Fuller's Camp, said Mr. Love is hereby entitled to all privileges accruing to guests of the camp as prescribed in the rules published by the owners, including the right to guest passes good for the use of the premises at Blaney Lodge as set out in the reciprocal agreement between the aforesaid Charles Fuller and the owners of Blaney Lodge. Signed, Martha Fuller. Her mark, X."

That last little touch went right over Mrs. Fuller's head. She could write, of course, and she signed her name, but I insisted on the X and she put it down. At the last minute, Mr. Jackson came down the stairs and I made him witness the document. When we got out on the porch he was smiling broadly.

"If you don't mind," he said to me, "I'd like a copy of that."

I caught three more pike before noon and, once again, having nothing to do, I decided to make the long trip into Germfask to see about the ring gear. I was almost halfway into town when Jean MacKenzie's roadster came up behind me and this time, lo and behold, she stopped.

"Want a lift?" she said.

"Sure," I said, and hopped into the seat beside her.

"What are you doing walking?" she asked me as she put the car in gear.

"I'm taking my exercise. I'm a demon walker."

"What about your pretty car? You wouldn't catch me walking if I had a car like that."

"Oh, that! My partner borrowed it. He wanted to go fishing for trout somewhere over near Newberry. He'll probably be back tonight. Exercise is good for you. I see you've been out horseback riding."

She looked down at her jodhpurs. "Oh, don't get me

wrong. I like exercise. I spend all summer exercising. I guess we have a lot in common."

"Yeah," I said. "Maybe we ought to exercise together."

"Do you ever go horseback riding?"

"I went horseback riding once. I took the whole Michigan football team horseback riding and they almost got beat by Chicago. No more horseback riding for me."

"Is that where you go to college? Michigan?"

"Yep."

"I go to Northwestern."

"Small world, isn't it?"

"Seriously, maybe we ought to do something together. What other sports do you like to play?"

"Baseball," I said.

"I think you're pulling my leg. I can't play baseball."

"How about swimming?" I said. "Maybe we could go swimming together."

"Oh, I like to swim. There's a good pool down at Blaney Lodge. Do you want to try it?"

"I wasn't exactly thinking of going swimming at Blaney Lodge," I said. "It seems kind of silly going swimming in a pool when there's a nice big lake around."

"You mean Big Manistique? Have you been swimming in the lake yet?"

"No."

"Well, you try it sometime. You'll freeze your— Well, you'll freeze. The water is really cold."

"I'm not afraid of cold water. Of course, if you are, then we'll have to swim in the Blaney pool."

"You don't know who you're talking to," she said. "I didn't say I was afraid of cold water. I'll tell you what I'll do with you. You try Big Manistique. You try it just once. If you survive, you come back and tell me and I'll go swimming with you out there. I'll take you to a nice little place I know."

"Now we're getting someplace," I said. I stuck out my

hand and she shook it. "In the meantime, how about doing something non-athletic?"

"Maybe we can get together," she said. "You try me."

We came into Germfask and she let me out in front of the post office. There was no mail, but that fact didn't bother me at all. I was beginning to enjoy myself and I don't think I was in any hurry for that ring gear to show up.

As I said, that was Wednesday. It was the night that George came down to the tent and told me he didn't think he'd be able to make it through until Saturday. It was peculiar that he would have said that right then, because I was suddenly having somewhat the same idea in another field. At dinner that evening, I first began to notice something peculiar about the fish I was eating. That was the fourth day in a row that I'd had fish for supper and I found myself debating for a long time before each bite.

Thursday was a day of disaster. At least I thought of it as a day of disaster during the early part of the day. My chance meeting with Jean MacKenzie had started me to thinking about her with some concentration and I'm afraid I thought about her all night long. The next morning, when I watched her take her dip, the ritual was almost too much for me. The thought that I might soon be a part of that little scene was overpowering. I began building a nice little fantasy about how the whole thing was going to work out and I rehearsed it several times. All the time I was off in dreamland, I was out in the boat trying to catch my daily fish. I was so preoccupied that I didn't pay much attention to the business in hand and I doubt whether fish are really interested in fishermen who have sex on their minds. They demand full attention. I stayed in one spot for two hours without getting so much as a nibble and then I picked up the oars and rowed farther out into the lake. At the second place I stopped I caught a nice pike, but after an hour without another bite, I decided to move again. By one o'clock I was way out in the middle of the lake. I had just finished pulling in my second catch when I heard the sound of an outboard motor approaching. I looked up and there was Charlie Fuller, not a hundred yards away. He turned off his motor and glided toward me.

"Where did you get that boat, boy?" he said.

"I found it in the bushes."

"I've been looking for that boat for almost a year."

"You couldn't have looked very hard," I said. "I didn't have any trouble finding it at all. Is it yours?"

"You know it's mine. I ought to have you arrested for stealing it."

"How could I have stolen it, Mr. Fuller? You said it's been missing a year. I wasn't within four hundred miles of here a year ago. If you ask me, you ought to give me a reward for finding it. Something like two months' free rent or something."

"Don't get smart with me, boy. You just get that boat over to the dock as quick as you can."

There wasn't anything else I could do. After Charlie left me he went back and stood on the end of his dock watching every move I made. If I'd tried to take it back to my bushes he would have seen exactly where I went. I just rowed in and turned the boat over to him. I spent the afternoon doing some laundry and then cleaned the fish. During the whole time I felt badly about losing the boat and I wondered what I was going to do now. It wasn't until I sat down to supper that I came to look on the whole thing as a blessing in disguise. I could hardly get the fish down. I ended up congratulating myself on the loss of the boat because now I wouldn't have to eat any more fish. That Thursday night, incidentally, was the night that George dropped off to sleep in his room. When he didn't show up by eight o'clock I went looking for him. I didn't find him, but I did run into Mr. Jackson sitting on the porch. He introduced me to his wife, an attractive, well-dressed young woman of about thirty. They invited me into the house to play a new game they'd just found. It turned out to be Monopoly. I enjoyed it except that Charlie Fuller played with us. He played for keeps and he ended up winning all the money and all the property.

The next morning was disappointing. I went over to my grandstand at the appointed time, but Jean MacKenzie didn't show up. I sat in those bushes for three hours before giving up. I decided that I'd better hurry into Germfask and see if anything had happened to her. It wasn't like her to miss that morning swim any more than it was like me to miss watching her. I got a ride part way, both ways, and I solved the mystery. I went into Alec MacKenzie's store and asked the lady who ran the place what had happened.

"She went down to St. Ignace to get her grandpa. They'll probably be back home after supper. You can call her on the telephone."

I recall that I was quite surprised to receive that information about the telephone. I suddenly realized that I hadn't heard a telephone ring for two whole weeks. I think I had come to think of Germfask as a place which didn't have any such contrivance. When I got back to Charlie Fuller's camp that evening, I began looking around the store to see if he had a phone. There didn't seem to be any so I went looking for George. I found him sweeping out the boathouse.

"Sure," he said. "Charlie's got a phone. It's one of those old-fashioned kinds that has a crank on the side of it. It's in the kitchen."

"Is it a pay phone?"

"Nope. You just make your call and give Mrs. Fuller a quarter. I saw somebody do it this morning."

"A quarter? Every place else it's a nickel."

"You know what Charlie says. I got the phone. If you want to use it, you pay my prices."

"Damn Charlie. He's everything they say about him. Someday, somehow, I'm going to beat him at his own game."

"I know how to do it," George said.

"How?"

He pointed at the slot machine. "About an hour ago a fellow came in here and put a nickel in that thing and three oranges came up. Charlie was really mad about that. We were filling up the outboards with gas and all the time we were working Charlie was muttering about how people were coming in here and winning his money. When we got done with the motors he got his screwdriver out and went over and took the back off the machine. He set it so that it won't pay off anything at all—not a nickel. I stood right beside him and watched him do it. You know what? I watched exactly which things he turned. I'm pretty sure I could take the back off that and turn the same gadgets and make it pay out good. Do you want to try it?"

"Now?"

"Sure. Charlie just took some people out fishing about an hour ago. He won't be back until suppertime."

"All right," I said. "Let's try it."

George went over and got a screwdriver and took the back off the machine and began tinkering around with the inside. When he was done he motioned to me and I put a nickel in the slot and pulled the lever. I got two cherries and a bar and two nickels dropped into the cup at the bottom. I put the two nickels in and got four back. I put the four nickels in and on the last one I hit three bells which gave me sixteen nickels. I had used about half of them up when I hit the jackpot.

"That's enough," I told George. "Set it back where it was and put the back back on."

"There's a whole tray of nickels in there," George said. "We might just as well help ourselves while we have this cover off."

"That's stealing, George," I said. "No."

"What the hell do you think you've been doing?"

"Doing it the way we did doesn't bother my conscience. Somehow I *feel* honest."

George reset the machine while I split up the swag. I had a dollar and fifteen cents in nickels for myself.

"I think I'll go up to the store and buy some bacon and bread with this."

George shook his head. "You can't. This is Friday. Mrs. Fuller took Charlie's truck and went over to Manistique this morning to do the weekly shopping. The store is closed while she's gone and she won't be back until seven o'clock. Anyway, you don't have to worry." He went out the door of the boathouse and came back in a moment with three fish dripping water. "I took some people out in a boat this morning and I caught these. I knew you didn't have any way of fishing any more so I saved them for you."

I groaned. "Honest, George, I don't know whether I could eat another fish if my life depended on it. What I'd really like right now is a pork chop. I sure wish I knew where I could get one."

"Why don't you go over to the A & P store in Newberry? I heard that Mr. Jackson talking at lunch today. He said he was going to drive over to Newberry and pick up his films in the morning. You could probably get a ride over with him and back."

I found Mr. Jackson restringing a fishing reel on the front porch of the big house.

"Sure," he said, "I'd be glad to give you a ride over to Newberry. The only thing is that I don't know how you'd get home again. Sally and I decided to make a day of it. We're not going over there until afternoon and then, instead of coming home, we're going down to Blaney Lodge and have dinner and go to the dance."

"I guess I could walk home from Germfask. I do it all the time."

"If you're sure you don't mind, you're welcome to come with us. You're even welcome to come down to Blaney with us if you want to, but I don't think we'll be coming home until two or three o'clock in the morning."

"Do you really mean that?"

"Sure."

"I might just take you up on it. I think I know where I can get a date."

I ate fish for supper. I give the credit for it to Jean Mac-Kenzie. I almost had to hold my nose to get it down, but I kept telling myself that it would be the last one I'd have to eat for a while. The next night I'd eat at Blaney Lodge and after that for a few days, I'd be having pork chops. Things really seemed to be looking up.

I began getting ready for my date with great gusto. I fished my suitcase out of the back of the car and laid out some clean clothes. Then I took a bar of soap and headed for Jean MacKenzie's cove. There I stripped and dove into the water. I jumped right back out again. Never in my life have I ever felt water as cold as that water was. I think that if it had been two degrees colder there would have been ice floating on top of it. I looked across to the other shore and I remembered how Jean looked diving in there every morning and I decided if she could do it, I could do it. I soaped myself all over and then took a deep breath and dove in the water again. I managed to stay in long enough to get the soap all off, but that was all I could stand. When I got back to my tent my teeth were still chattering. I'll say one thing. I had great respect for Jean MacKenzie.

By the time I finished bathing, there were lights up in the big house and I could see Charlie's old truck parked around to the side so I knew that Mrs. Fuller had got back from her shopping expedition. I walked in and asked her if I could use the phone—I would pay for it. After she said yes, I looked around for the phone book.

"We don't have any telephone book," Mrs. Fuller said. "We don't need any. I know everybody's phone number for forty miles around here. Who do you want to call?"

"Jean MacKenzie."

She glared at me. "Not on this phone you don't."

"This is a public telephone, isn't it?"

"It's not that public." She flounced out of the room.

I went looking for George and told him about it. I didn't get much sympathy.

"I don't know why you're wasting your time on that girl anyway. For once I think Mrs. Fuller is right."

"Now look here," I said, "I don't tell you who to date and who not to date and I don't expect you to tell me. You don't hear me complaining about that girl you have over in Curtis, do you?"

"I certainly did hear you complaining. You were even going to walk out on me."

"I wasn't complaining about the girl. I was complaining about the money you spent."

"Same thing." He shook his head. "If you really want to talk to her, why don't you go over and talk to her when she goes swimming in the morning?"

"George, I couldn't do that. How could I? What do you say to a naked girl?"

Actually, as it turned out, I needn't have worried about *that*. For the second morning in a row, Jean didn't show up at the old swimming hole. I moped around the camp all morning with absolutely nothing to do. I didn't eat anything, either. I was out of everything but fish and I couldn't stand it to even look at those. At a little after two o'clock in the afternoon I got all dressed up in the only shirt and tie I had brought along on the trip. The Jacksons and I arrived in Newberry around five in the afternoon and I spent my slot machine winnings in the A & P store. I bought a half dozen pork chops. I also bought a little more bacon, some bread, and a box of ZuZu gingersnaps. I hadn't had any candy or sweets of any kind since I left home and the gingersnaps appealed to me.

On the way back, the Jacksons agreed to wait in Germfask

while I asked Jean MacKenzie for a date. They sat in the car while I climbed up the steps and knocked on the front door of the house in the pines. I got no answer so I went back over to MacKenzie's store.

"You're out of luck, sonny boy," the lady in the store said. "Jean and her grandfather didn't come home. The old man had some business over at the Soo so they're going to stay over there for the weekend. I expect them back on Monday."

The Jacksons kindly offered to take me along with them to Blaney anyway, but I declined. I wasn't quite ready, yet, to spend any money except in a good cause. I watched them drive off down the road and then I started for home. That was a long and lonely walk. I didn't arrive at the tent until well after dark. There I found a note from George. He'd completed his week's work for Charlie Fuller and had been paid. He'd gone off to Curtis to see his girl. Once again I was all alone on a Saturday night and the camp seemed deserted. I built up the fires and cooked three of the pork chops. After dinner I took all my food except the ginger-snaps over to the icehouse and hid it away in the little cache that George and I had made for ourselves after the porcupine incident. I ended the evening by sitting in front of the fire eating gingersnaps. When George hadn't arrived home by midnight, I put the remaining gingersnaps on the picnic table and went to bed.

I didn't sleep very long. It couldn't have been more than an hour. I woke up with a start, knowing instinctively that someone or something was moving around outside the tent. As I lay there, trying to get my bearings, my first thought was that George had come home drunk, but after a moment or two I realized that whatever was out there was making a peculiar snorting and grunting noise. I was very cautious. I had no intention of getting mixed up with any more porcupines. I slowly edged around so that I could peek out under the flap. There at the picnic table, about thirty feet away, was a big, black bear. I could just make him out in the faint glow from the dying embers of my campfire. He had his forepaws up on the picnic table, holding the box of gingersnaps while he rooted in it in obvious pleasure. It's a funny thing about bears. There is something so big and lovable about them that the average human being just has no fear of them. When I first saw this one I was inclined to relax, but something told me I hadn't better. The only person in my whole life who'd ever had anything to do with a bear was my grandfather who had once shot one while on a hunting expedition.

"I got him with one shot," Grandpa had told me. "That's a good thing to remember. You'd better get them on the first shot because you might never get a second shot. There's nothing meaner in the world than a wounded bear."

While I watched that bear devouring those gingersnaps I came to the conclusion that he might feel the same way about being separated from them as he would if he was shot. I didn't have a gun, of course, and the only other tidbit of information I had about wild animals had been dug out of James Oliver Curwood's books that I had read when I was young. In those the hero was always throwing logs on the fire to keep wild animals at bay. I decided that's what I'd better do. I carefully reached an arm out of the tent and managed to get hold of three or four sticks of firewood which I had piled nearby. The bear was still busy with the gingersnaps and hadn't noticed me at all. Taking careful aim I tossed a stick at the fire. It landed in the embers with a big plop and sparks flew in all directions. The bear turned his head and looked straight at me. I threw another stick and more sparks flew. The bear dropped down to the ground and faced me on all fours. I threw another stick and he began moving his head from side to side and I heard an ominous growl. I think I was in real trouble at that moment, but Providence took a hand. The first stick I had thrown suddenly burst into bright flame. The bear was obviously startled by this: He growled again and then raised up on his hind legs and made a pawing motion in the air. The next thing I knew he was gone. He moved so quickly that I didn't see him go. I stayed there, half on my knees. I think I was waiting for him to jump on me from the back. It was a long time before I dared to move. When I did move I threw another stick on the fire, then another. The fire was beginning to burn brightly now, and I kept throwing more wood on it. I soon had a roaring blaze that lit up the woods for yards around me. I kept it roaring all through the rest of that night. I never moved more than five feet away from it.

About an hour after I woke up I saw the headlights of a car come up the road and stop in front of the big house. I was pretty sure it was the Jacksons and I thought of running up the hill and trying to warn them that there was a bear in the neighborhood, but I debated too long about going out there in the dark where the bear might be and long before I got up the courage, I saw the lights go on and I knew that the Jacksons had gotten inside safely. When it finally began to get light in the east, and not until then, I crawled back into the tent and lay down and went back to sleep.

It must have been nine o'clock that Sunday morning when I was awakened by someone pulling on my leg. I opened my eyes slowly and looked for the bear. He wasn't there, but Charlie Fuller was.

"Where's that good-for-nothing buddy of yours?" he asked.

"How should I know? He doesn't have to work on Sundays, does he?"

"No. He doesn't have to work on Sunday, but I told him last night that I had some people who'd need a fishing guide this morning if he wanted to make an extra dollar. Do you want to earn a dollar?"

"I don't know anything about fishing. I certainly don't know enough to be a guide."

"You don't have to know anything. You just go where I tell you to go and you'll catch plenty of fish."

"All right," I said.

I didn't even take the time to eat breakfast. I just threw on some old clothes and headed for the fishing dock. I was a little unprepared for what I found down there. On Sundays Charlie Fuller's camp resembled a county fair. People from towns all over the upper peninsula streamed in for a day of fishing. Charlie, himself, was playing a regular tune on the cash register in the boathouse. Mrs. Fuller was out on the dock with a clipboard, checking out boats. Even Charlie's daughters, who ranged from six to eleven years of age, were busy. They were selling box lunches at a little stand near the shore end of the dock. People were milling around, flicking fishing rods, comparing flies, looking at each other's equipment. Several people were busy attaching outboard motors to the backs of boats. I wandered around in the midst of this crowd for several minutes and then Charlie saw me. He came out from behind his cash register, grabbed me by the arm, and led me out onto the dock. He pointed off toward my grandfather's property, three miles away. There was a little island there, a hundred yards off-shore.

"You go over there about fifty yards east of that island. That's where the fish should be this morning," he said. "As long as you stay in that area, you'll catch them. If they stop biting, just hold up your finger and see which way the wind is blowing. Move about a half mile with the wind."

After showing me where the fish were, he took me over to a boat and introduced me to a rather elderly couple who were loading things into it. They had two big metal boxes full of fishing tackle, two big picnic baskets, and all kinds of raincoats, sun hats, and other extra clothing. By the time they got all this in the boat, and got themselves in, I thought the thing was going to sink. They sat there, looking up at me expectantly.

"Come on, boy!" the man said, impatiently. "Let's get going."

I looked along the dock where everyone else seemed to be winding up outboard motors. "Am I supposed to row this thing?" I asked.

"If you want your dollar, you will," the man said.

I got in and unshipped the oars and pushed off. With all that weight in the boat it was hard going. By the time we'd crossed three miles of water to the spot Charlie had pointed out, my back had begun to ache. I stopped rowing and we all baited our hooks. Even though I'd reached the point where I couldn't look a fish in the face, I'd brought along my own fishing rod. There might be some emergency in which it would be a good thing to have a fish on hand. I managed to get my hook baited and my line in the water first that morning. The old man hadn't even made his cast yet when I had a strike. Before I had my fish out of the water, the old man had a bite. Before he landed his catch, his wife had a fish on the line. For the next hour we pulled fish out of that lake as fast as we could bait our hooks and cast. The more fish we caught the more the old man muttered.

"I don't call this fishing," he said finally, in some disgust. "I like to feel like I've worked for my fish. Find another place where they don't bite so good."

I put down my rod and held my finger in the air to see which way the wind was blowing. It was coming from the east, so I rowed east, just the opposite of what Charlie had told me to do. I rowed for a good half hour, for a mile or better. When I stopped and made my first cast at the new place, I caught another fish at once. The old man and his wife caught five in rapid succession. The old man threw his hat in the bottom of the boat.

"Goddamn it, boy!" he shouted at me. "Move again, will you? This time go someplace where there aren't so many fish."

I rowed some more. I rowed across the lake and I rowed

back again. I rowed up the lake and I rowed down again. Every place we stopped the fish almost jumped in the boat. I finally came creeping into Charlie's dock about five in the afternoon with blistered hands and a back that felt like it was broken. I had thirty fish of my own and the old man and his wife had more than a hundred between them. As far as I was concerned, there had been only one enjoyable moment in that whole day. That had come around one o'clock when the old lady opened the picnic baskets and handed me three ham sandwiches. To hear the old couple talk it had been the worst day of fishing in their whole life, but they paid me my dollar and I took my string of fish and trudged off to my tent. When I got there I found George eating the last of my pork chops.

"Where do you get off eating those pork chops?" I yelled at him.

"That was all the food I could find, except bacon," he said.

"I know, but you're supposed to be eating up at the house."

"I quit. I was going to tell you last night, but you didn't get here before I left for Curtis. I wouldn't work for that slave driver up there for another day for all the rice in China."

"Somebody's got to work for him. How are we going to pay for this camping place?"

"I thought you were going to move over to MacKenzie's place."

"I intend to, but I don't know whether we can get this car moved or not."

"Well, if you want the job, it's open. But if you're going to work for Charlie, you'd better get up to the house right now. Mrs. Fuller rang the dinner bell ten minutes ago. Those dinners are the only part of the job you don't want to miss."

I looked down at that string of fish. I knew that George

had finished off the pork chops and that there wasn't much else to eat but a little bacon. It was just too much for me. I thrust the fish at him.

"They're all yours," I said. "I hope you choke on them. I'll take the job."

TWELVE

I don't think Charlie Fuller was happy to see me when I walked in on him that Sunday evening. He and the family and the guests, including the Jacksons, were all gathered around the big dining-room table.

"I heard you had a job open," I said.

"Yeah. Your good-for-nothing side-kick walked out on me. I need a hired man, but I don't think I want you."

"Have it your own way," I said and turned to go.

"Wait a minute," he said. "I'll take you, but I'll only pay you two-fifty."

"Mr. Fuller, I'm the only available hired man around here right now. Like you say, if you want to do business with me, you pay my prices. My price is four-fifty a week."

I think Charlie was over a barrel and I think he knew it. Besides that, I had Mr. Jackson to bat for me. I think Mr. Jackson told him he was pretty foolish to let me get away. At any rate, I was almost back down at the tent when one of the back windows of the house went up and Charlie shouted at me.

"I'll give you three-fifty, not a penny more," he yelled.

I walked back up to the house, re-entered, and Charlie

waved a fork at a vacant chair and told me to sit down. Mrs. Fuller went out into the kitchen and returned with a heaping plate of roast beef hash. In all my life I'd never been very fond of hash, but that hash tasted delicious. Anything that didn't have fins on it would have tasted delicious.

From the moment I rose from that supper table, my memory becomes hazy. I wasn't exactly a neophyte when it came to hard work. I'd spent two years driving a coal truck and I could stand backbreaking labor. There was plenty of it at Charlie's place, but the thing that made working for him so awful was the fact that there was never any respite. The days began at daylight and the work was never finished until long after dark. The variety and the number of chores was endless. And Charlie wasn't in the least bit organized. He just did things as he thought of them. Some of the time I worked with him and some of the time I worked alone, but always by the time I had finished one job, he'd thought up the next one. At some time during that week, George stopped by where I was hoeing potatoes in the garden to ask me a question. Charlie was way down in the barn and he stuck his head out the door and hollered.

"Get away from that boy and stop bothering him. I'm not paying him to lollygag around talking to good-for-nothing loafers."

That label of "good-for-nothing" was used over and over again. He would say, "Hurry up, you good-for-nothing kid," or "What's got into that good-for-nothing brain of yours?" The mere fact that Charlie worked every bit as hard as I did, that he always seemed to move from one chore to another at a trot, didn't make me admire him any more. It made me hate him.

On that Sunday night he gave me ten minutes to go down to the tent and bring up my belongings. He showed me into a cubicle in the basement that had a bed in it and not much else. After I'd put my things down he took me outside of the cubicle and showed me a shower and a sink and a toilet that I could use. I didn't see them again until midnight because we went to work. Two new sets of guests were expected and I had to open the cabins. Opening a cabin consisted of carrying several armloads of wood up from the sawmill, putting fifty-pound chunks of ice in the refrigerators, and sweeping out. After the cabins were opened I had to go down to the docks and carry in all the outboard motors from the boats and put them in their racks in the boathouse. Then I had to bring in eggs and wood for Mrs. Fuller's kitchen in the big house. I was already tired from rowing a boat all day and when I did fall into bed I slept like a log. I was up promptly at four-thirty the next morning. Before I ever had a bite of breakfast I had milked twenty cows, turned them out to pasture, and carried three thirty-gallon cans of milk up to the house. Every day was the same from morning until night.

George had been so tired during the week he worked for Charlie that he had scarcely bothered to walk down to the tent to see what I was doing. By noon of my second day I found that I couldn't care less what was happening outside of my own little world. Although I drove the cattle out to pasture every morning I never once walked over the next little hill to see if Jean MacKenzie had come back to her morning dip. I must have gone down to the tent at various times, but I have little memory of it. I do know that I went down there once and found a note on the table saying that George had gone over to Curtis to see his girl, but I have the impression that it had been written the day before and that George was gone off for two or three days. At some time in the middle of the week he came down to the icehouse where I was cutting ice and I asked him if the ring gear for the car had showed up yet. To my utter disgust I learned that he hadn't been near Germfask once and I told him what I thought of him. Toward the end of the week, when I saw him again, he complained about both the mosquitoes and the fact that he was tired of eating fish. For some reason or other that pleased me no end.

Of all the things that disillusioned both of us, I suppose it was that steady, unchanging diet of fish. I had already begun to realize that our expedition would probably fail because of that one thing. Fortunately, on the next to the last day of that first week I worked for Charlie, I found a happy solution to it. I'd been told to put ice in all the refrigerators that morning. When I came into Cabin Four, however, I found Mrs. Wells bustling about.

"We don't need that ice this morning," she said. "We're going home. I've already cleaned out the icebox." She pointed at a pile of groceries sitting there on the kitchen table. I went over and looked at it. There was a full loaf of bread and almost a pound of bacon among the other things on that table.

"Are you going to throw all this away?" I asked.

"I just leave it there and Charlie comes and gets it. I guess he uses it up at the big house."

"Boy, I could sure use that bacon," I said.

"You might just as well have it as Charlie. Take the whole works if you want it."

I rushed next door and delivered my ice, then stopped back and scooped up the whole pile of groceries and carried it back down to the little hiding place George and I had fashioned for ourselves in the icehouse. Not very long after this happened, Charlie informed me that Cabin Ten was also checking out that morning. He ordered me to scrub it out. When I walked in the back door I found another pile of groceries sitting on the kitchen table. I left them sitting there, intending to grab them up after I had finished my scrubbing. I never had a chance to appropriate them, however. While I was still on my hands and knees Charlie hurried in, put everything in a cardboard box, and carried it off. Ten minutes later, as I went down the hill past Mrs. Wells's cabin, I heard him in the kitchen banging cupboard doors and slamming drawers shut. Suddenly he stuck his head out the door and yelled at me.

"Hey, boy! Have you seen anyone hanging around this cabin?"

"Nope. Why?"

"Somebody stole the groceries she was going to leave for me."

"Maybe the good-for-nothing woman didn't leave them," I said.

Maybe nothing would have come from all this if I hadn't taken ice up to the big house a few minutes later. When I walked into the kitchen I could look through the door into the store. There was Charlie, carefully putting the eggs and bread and bacon and butter from Cabin Ten into the store's stock. That was when I knew why he was selling bacon and bread by the slice. Not only that. That tightwad was probably selling everything twice. Maybe even three times for all I knew. I was mad clear through and I kept getting madder the longer the day lasted. By the time I went to bed that night I'd made up my mind that he'd sold his last leftover to people like me. I was going to beat him to every batch of groceries that was left behind. The next morning when I made my daily ice delivery, I carefully checked with each tenant to find out exactly when they intended to check out.

I didn't have a chance to use this information myself because that Saturday was the last day I worked for Charlie. Nevertheless, I was the beneficiary of it. My relationship with Charlie, despite the fact that I was quite disgusted with him by the end of the week, had been passable. I had done all the work that he had given me to do. I think he was satisfied to keep me on for as long as I wanted to work. My trouble was with George.

George had taken the job as hired man in the first place because he wanted money, especially to spend on the girl he'd found in Curtis. When he had quit his job on the previous Saturday night he had evidently forgotten this small fact. We had now arrived at another Saturday and there would be another dance. Charlie had kept me working hard right up until suppertime. The last thing I did was to clean out all the boats so that they would be ready for the Sunday crowd. We were down at the boathouse and Charlie went over to the cash register and took out two dollar bills and handed them to me.

"I deducted your dollar and a half's rent," he said. "That's what you have coming. Don't spend it all in one place. Supper will be ready in twenty minutes."

I shoved the money in my pants pocket and wearily climbed the stairs to make my way to my little cubicle in the basement of the big house. I found George sitting on the bed, waiting for me.

"Did you get paid?" he asked me.

"Yeah. It wasn't much, but I got it."

"Well," George said, "I'd like to borrow a couple of dollars."

"You what?" I asked him.

"I want to borrow a couple of dollars. I have a date in Curtis."

I looked at him. I hadn't expected this at all. I wanted to be reasonable, but this was a little too much.

"George, if I give you two bucks, then I've worked this whole week for nothing. It's bad enough to work for Charlie for two dollars, but to work a whole week the way I did for nothing, that's just too much."

"Oh, come on!" he said. "Are we going through this all over again?"

"Oh, come on, yourself, George. I'm not going to break my back just so you can be an upper peninsula social butterfly."

"I don't think you're being very fair. You got me to come all the way up here with you. Now you won't even lend me any money so I can go and see my girl."

"You're the one that's not being fair," I said. "Look, George, you haven't lifted a goddamned finger all week. You spent three or four days running back and forth over to Curtis. You didn't even go into Germfask once to see if the ring gear was there yet. And what about that money you said your mother was going to send you? You didn't even go in to see if it came in the mail."

"Well, I was going to go in today, but I couldn't get a ride. I sat down there on the corner for two hours and not a single car went by."

"You could have walked," I said. "I walked."

He glared at me. "Then you're not going to give me the two bucks?"

"Nope."

He got to his feet and stormed out of the room. I went about getting washed up for supper and then went upstairs. Before I sat down to my meal, I looked out the back window. I think I half expected to see him pulling his stuff out of the car. But even if I'd seen him doing that I don't think I would have tried to stop him. I was fed up. The fact that he wasn't down there going through the motions of packing proved one thing. He wasn't going home. He was going to Curtis.

The Jacksons had spent the day over in the iron country and at dinner that evening they announced that they were too tired to go out. They wanted to know if I'd be interested in another game of Monopoly. So, along with two of the other guests and Charlie, we sat up in the big dining room and played. George didn't have any luck in Curtis at all. He'd arrived over there without any money. His girl liked him well enough, I suppose, but she didn't like him well enough to pay his way into the dance. George came dragging back into the camp around midnight and when I went to bed I could see him down there sitting in front of the tent staring into the fire.

The next morning, bright and early, George was down

at the dock asking Charlie if anyone needed a fishing guide. Charlie steered him to a man who hired him. He not only got the dollar fee as a guide, but he got a dollar tip as well. I had a guiding job that Sunday morning, too. This one turned out to be a lot better than the first time I tried it because this time my man had an outboard motor and he was willing to call it quits around one in the afternoon. I went up to my room and stretched out on my bed to take a nap because I knew the week's work would begin with a vengeance the minute supper was over with. When I woke up I found George sitting on the little camp chair at the foot of my bed.

"I want to ask you a favor," he said and then hastily added, "I don't want to borrow any money."

"Go ahead," I said.

"Well, I was wondering if it would be all right with you if I took the job back. I can sure use the money." He sighed a big sigh.

"I suppose you're tired of eating fish, too?"

"I hope I never see another fish as long as I live."

"I don't like them, either."

"I know, but you've had a whole week without them. And you've got enough money in your pocket so that you can buy some more pork chops."

"George, I'm certainly not in love with this job and I have an idea how to keep from eating fish every meal, but the thing is, what's Charlie going to say if you tell him you're taking my place? I don't think he's going to like it very well if you and I keep switching back and forth all the time."

"I already asked Charlie about it. He don't care which one of us works as long as one of us does. He said it's up to you."

"It's a wonder he didn't try to reduce our wages what with the two of us fighting over his lousy job."

"He didn't say anything about that."

"Well, don't let him. I'll make a deal with you, George.

If you'll promise to do what I say, I'll let you have the job."

"What do you want me to do?"

"Well, Friday I put a bag of groceries down in the icehouse for you. They came from Cabin Four. I found out that most of these people leave the stuff they don't want to cart home with them. Charlie gets it and puts it up in the store and sells it again to suckers like us. Some of them leave some pretty good things. I went around yesterday morning and I made a list of exactly when all these people will be leaving. I'll give it to you. What I want you to do is to get to these cabins before Charlie does. Just get all the groceries they leave and put them in the icehouse or wherever I can find them. I ought not to have to eat fish more than once or twice this week."

"All right," he said, "I'll do it."

THIRTEEN

Having had one week of sleeping in a bed, I had all but forgotten what it was like down in that tent of ours. On that Sunday evening while I fought off the mosquitoes and sat in front of my campfire, I began to take stock of the situation. It was now August 11. We had been gone from home for three weeks. In that pell-mell week of rushing from one of Charlie's backbreaking jobs to another, so many things had receded into the background that the whole original idea of our trip had been completely discarded. We'd found my grandfather's property and we'd had a look at it. It was impossible to camp on it. It seemed that the sensible thing to do was sell it, but the only person who had expressed an interest in it was Alec MacKenzie and I hadn't seen him since that first brief encounter. Our money had all but run out. It was true that with the money I'd made working for Charlie I was now almost back up at the ten-dollar mark, but I knew that would dwindle. It just wasn't worth it to stay up there any longer. The only reason we were staying was that old car. The thing to do was get it repaired and get it out of there and go home. The second most important thing to do was to go and see Alec MacKenzie and see just what he would offer, then make a deal. I decided, somewhat typically, to attack our problems systematically. First things first. I would begin by going in to Germfask the next morning. There I would pick up the ring gear. Once that was in hand, I would look up Alec MacKenzie and get the property matter settled. I went to bed full of vim and vigor and determination. When I woke up in the morning I started right out by doing the natural thing. I went over to the cove to see if Jean MacKenzie had returned to normal. She had. She was going swimming in the same old way. I promptly added one other thing to my agenda. I was going to do something about her.

That little expedition to the cove was the only auspicious thing that happened to me that first day I rejoined the ranks of the unemployed. When I started for Germfask, I found the road devoid of traffic. I had to walk every foot of the way into town and every foot of the way back so that it was almost four o'clock in the afternoon before I got back. There was no ring gear. There was no letter from George's mother. There was nothing but a big fat silence. I did stop by MacKenzie's store to ask if Alec was there. I was informed that he was out at the camp. He would be out there all week. I asked for Jean. The lady said that she was playing in a ladies' golf tournament down at Blaney Lodge. All of this added up to one big fat gob of frustration.

When I got back to the camp that afternoon, I turned my attention to food. I knew that Cabin Eight had been vacated that morning and I wondered whether George had followed my instructions about the food. He had. When I went over to the icehouse and looked into our little hiding place, I found a great big bag of groceries. George had made a good haul, indeed. There was the usual bacon, some bread, several eggs, a half pound of hamburger meat, some frankfurters, a quart of milk, and some apples. The most interesting item in this collection of odds and ends, however, was a box of something called Bisquick. In this day and age, when we are used to seeing the shelves of grocery stores loaded down with boxes of prepared mixes, it is important to recall that 1934 was still relatively innocent of this kind of thing. About the only mix that I'd ever heard of at that time was Aunt Jemima pancake mix. I'd certainly never heard of Bisquick and the fact that there was something which could produce biscuits simply by adding water was an intriguing discovery. I sat there on a cake of ice and looked the package over and then took it back to my tent with me. I planned a really fine meal for that evening—a sort of upper peninsula broil that consisted of bacon, frankfurters and hamburger all cooked together. To top it all off I thought I'd have some biscuits made from the Bisquick box. This involved a major engineering project. I had to have some kind of an oven. I went to work digging out a big hole in the ground. When it was scooped out, I scrambled around gathering rocks. I cemented these together with a mortar I concocted out of the available mud, sand, and water. I went over to Charlie's rubbish heap and dug out several large tin cans, cut the tops off them and flattened them out with a hammer to make shelves and a top for my baking chamber. When I finished all of this I was quite proud of my handiwork. It looked like a very compact and serviceable oven.

It was at this point, I think, that I really sat down to read the printing on the box of Bisquick. To my utter pleasure I discovered that biscuits weren't the only thing I could make from the contents of that box. By adding an egg and a cup of milk—instead of water—I could make muffins. I was very fond of muffins. Since I was a small boy, muffins had been a staple of our Sunday-morning breakfast table at home. Indeed, muffins were the things that made Sunday-morning breakfasts different from all the others. In reading the instructions on that box, it seemed to be as easy to make muffins as it was to make biscuits. Furthermore, I had eggs and milk. And during the previous week, when I'd been scrubbing out the cabins, one of the things I'd noticed was that there were muffin tins hanging on the wall in almost every kitchen. Without any hesitation, I scurried across to the cabin area and knocked on one of the cabin doors and asked the lady who answered if I could borrow a muffin tin.

I mixed up the batch of muffins and poured them in the tin. Then I built a roaring fire under my oven and stuck the muffin tin in on one of the shelves. Alas! I wasn't very good at building ovens. Everything went well for a few minutes and then the heat from the fire dried out my mortar and the whole thing collapsed, muffins and all.

I had no intention of giving up my muffins at that point. I had set my appetite rheostat for muffins and I was going to have them. I fished the muffin tin out of the fire and washed it, then made up another batch. This time I carried my tin up to the big house where I knew there was always a big fire going in the kitchen range. When I came into the kitchen I found Mrs. Fuller and her oldest daughter moving about getting ready for supper as they always did at that hour. There were several pans simmering on the top of the stove.

"Mrs. Fuller," I said, "are you baking anything in the oven right now?"

"No. Everything is done. Why?"

"Well, I just made a batch of muffins, but the oven I built won't work. I was wondering, as long as you've got a fire going, whether I could pop them in."

I didn't realize it, but I had just made a startling statement. I had invaded a woman's world.

"You made some muffins?" Mrs. Fuller looked at me in astonishment. "I don't believe it."

I thrust the tin at her. She seemed to be afraid to touch it. She stood there wiping her hands on her apron and shaking her head. I think I could have produced the same effect if I'd told her that I'd discovered her youngest daughter taking boxing lessons. Everything in her background told her that men couldn't possibly make a batch of muffins. I thrust the tin at her again. Timidly she reached out a hand and took it. She cocked her head and looked at it from one side and then cocked her head the other way and looked at it from the other side. Finally, she held it up to her nose and smelled it. I half expected her to say "Hmmmmmph," but she didn't. She fluffed her apron at me.

"Go sit down in a corner and stay out of my way," she said. "I'll take care of these." She turned around and opened the oven door and slid the tin in on the top shelf.

I did as I was told. I retired to a remote corner and found a stool and climbed up on it to watch. The whole atmosphere of that kitchen had changed. Charlie's mother-in-law came in to help serve the evening meal and I saw the two women whispering in the doorway, every now and then stopping to cast a glance at the oven. Charlie's younger daughters fluttered in and after a sharp word and more whispers they began moving on tiptoe, stopping every few minutes to look first at me and then at the stove. Eventually, the testing began. First Mrs. Fuller, and then her mother, would take a straw out of the broom and go over and stick it in the muffins. That batch of Bisquick was certainly taking a beating and I began to have great admiration for it. At long last, with a great flourish, everyone gathered around and Mrs. Fuller bent over and used her apron to extract the tin from the oven. She put it up on top of the stove and stood there with her hands on her hips looking at those perfectly rounded little cones. She was so curious that her eyes were popping. The girls were almost jumping up and down. I climbed down from my stool and approached the gathering.

"Mrs. Fuller," I said. "Would you like to try one of those?"

"I certainly would!" she said. "I certainly would!"

I pried one out of the tin and handed it to her. Then I gave one to Charlie's mother-in-law and one to each of the girls. Mrs. Fuller carefully passed hers back and forth from one hand to the other, cooling it, measuring it, weighing it.

When it was cool enough she broke it open and spread a big dab of butter on it, then bit into it. By that time I was on tenterhooks myself. I watched anxiously as she chewed away and tossed it around judiciously in her mouth so as to get every speck of flavor out of it. Finally she blinked her eyes and nodded.

"Good!" she said. "Delicious! Absolutely delicious!" She looked up at me in approbation. "I wouldn't have believed it. I simply wouldn't have believed it." Suddenly, as though coming to a decision, she smiled. "I'd like to have that recipe."

That was a critical moment. If she hadn't been so superior and disdainful in the beginning, I think I would have told her the truth, that I got those muffins out of a Bisquick box. As it was, something in her manner told me that here was an art that I had mastered and she hadn't. I quickly made up my mind that I would be damned if I would tell her about the Bisquick. Of course, I had to do some pretty quick thinking to get around that sudden request for a recipe. What came out of my mouth was a little taller than even I expected.

"Mrs. Fuller," I said, "I can't give you that recipe. It's my mother's most precious secret. She sort of makes a living out of those muffins and if that recipe ever got out she might never be able to sell another muffin. Before she ever gave me that recipe, she made me promise her that I'd never reveal it."

Having uttered those stirring words, I grabbed up the tin of muffins and ducked for the door.

When I got down to the tent I found George poking around in the back of the car looking for something or other. I gave him one of the muffins and told him how I came by them. I also thought I'd better caution him not to give away the secret so I told him what I'd said to Mrs. Fuller when she asked me for the recipe. He thought it was pretty funny. He thought it was so funny that when he got up to the house for supper he elaborated on it. He told Mrs. Fuller that my poor old widowed mother made the best muffins in all of Michigan and that she'd brought up a whole family on the proceeds from them.

I had some immediate results. Mr. Jackson came strolling down to my tent and lit his pipe and sat down by the fire.

"I don't suppose you have any of those muffins left over, do you?"

"I'm sorry," I said. "I just ate the last one."

"I'm in the food business, you know. I think you just might have a good thing there. There's a fortune to be made in muffins."

"Not in these muffins," I said.

"You'd be surprised. I hope you are a wide-awake young man and that you know enough to take advantage of an opportunity when you see one."

"Now, look here, Mr. Jackson, if you knew—"

He held up his hand. "Don't give away your trade secrets," he said. "The reason I made money in the breakfast food business was because I never told anyone the recipe. That's the whole key to success. First you create a demand. Then you keep your mouth shut."

I didn't understand what he was talking about, but I found out the next morning. When I came back from my morning expedition to the cove, I found Mrs. Fuller sitting on the bench of our picnic table.

"How much does your mother get for a dozen of those muffins?" she said.

I had no idea what the going price for a dozen muffins would be, but I took a shot in the dark.

"Fifty cents," I said.

"No wonder she was able to put your sister through college," Mrs. Fuller said, getting up from the bench. "I was going to buy a dozen of them for the table up at the house. Mr. Jackson seems to think that we are entertaining an angel unawares. He knows about your mother. But fifty cents a dozen is too expensive for me."

"Well, Mrs. Fuller, my mother's customers are all pretty rich and they can afford it, but I guess I could make a compromise for you. If you'd promise to take a dozen for three or four days in a row, I think I could furnish them to you for twenty-five cents a dozen."

"At that price," she said, "I'll take a dozen every day for two weeks. We're going to be full up until Labor Day and I think my customers will like them. You deliver the first batch this afternoon."

That's how things were on that expedition. I kept getting sidetracked. I'd made up my mind to keep my eye on business. I'd planned to go over and see Alec MacKenzie at his camp that morning, and here I was in the muffin business. The minute that Mrs. Fuller went back up to the house I rushed for my food cache in the icehouse and retrieved the box of Bisquick. There was enough left in the box for one batch, but I had to steal a cup of milk from one of the cows in the pasture and I had to get a fresh egg out of the hen house. I managed to get the muffins—unbaked—to the kitchen in time for Mrs. Fuller to put them in the oven for lunch. After that it was nip and tuck. I began by having George inspect all the kitchens in the cabins when he made his daily ice delivery, but he couldn't find another box of Bisquick in the whole camp. About three in the afternoon, I ran into Mr. Jackson up on the common.

"I see business is prospering," he said.

"Oh, business is good enough," I said, "but I have a problem."

"Why don't you try the A & P store over in Newberry?" he said.

I scouted around the camp and found one of the guests who was planning to go trout fishing at Taquahmenon River the next morning so I got up at four o'clock and rode over with him. Taquahmenon was six miles from Newberry and I had to walk the whole six miles into town. The A & P store had four boxes of Bisquick on the shelf and I bought all four of them. They came to twenty-two cents apiece. I almost came to grief, however. It was a cold, blustery morning in the upper peninsula and there wasn't much traffic on the road that Wednesday morning. I didn't catch a ride back to Germfask until noon and then I had to walk all the way back out to the camp. It was after four o'clock when I finally walked into the kitchen with my new batch of muffins. Mrs. Fuller was quite upset because I was so late. I had to promise her to deliver them to her each morning at ten o'clock after that. I'd been so busy getting over to Newberry and back, incidentally, that I forgot to pay Charlie his weekly rent and when I got back down to the tent after delivering the muffins, I found him waiting for me.

"I thought you were going to take it out of our pay," I said. "George is working for you."

"He said he don't want me to. He says it's your car and you have to pay. He says you're in business now and you can afford it."

"That's George," I said. "He's as tight as some other people I know around here."

"That's funny. That's what he said about you. I believe him. I see you've been over to Newberry shopping. I'd call that being pretty tight, going all the way over there and back just to save paying my wife for doing your shopping for you."

"Your wife couldn't have found this in a hundred years."

"I wouldn't be too sure of that. What did you buy?"

The bag with the Bisquick in it was sitting there in plain sight on the table and he took a step toward it. I wasn't going to let him see that. I reached over in the front seat of the car and grabbed a can and held it up for him. He took it from me and turned it over and over.

"Monkey Tire Patch," he said. "I haven't seen any of that in twenty years. Where did you get it?"

"From an old Buick dealer. I got all he had."

"This used to be pretty good stuff," he said. "You didn't get an extra can of it did you?"

"I sure did," I said. "Do you want it?"

"How much?"

"A dollar and a half," I said.

"That's too much. I used to be able to get it for forty-seven cents."

"I got it, Charlie. That's all there is. If you want it, you pay my prices."

He kept looking at it, turning it over and over, occasionally stopping to look up at his old truck which was parked beside the house. "I don't know," he said.

"That will probably save you buying a new tire, maybe two new tires," I said. "Tires are expensive."

He nodded. "All right," he said. "Your rent is paid for this week, but you'll have to show my wife how to use it. She does all the driving around here." He stuck the can in his pocket and started up the hill.

"I'll give your daughters a lesson, too," I shouted after him. "And even your mother-in-law."

After he was out of sight I grabbed up the bag of Bisquick and headed for the icehouse. When I got there, I sat down for a moment to figure out where I stood financially. I was doing pretty well. Each box of Bisquick, according to the label, was good for six batches of muffins. That was a dollar and a half, a net profit of $1.28 a box.

"If this keeps up, we can live here practically forever," I told George when he came down to the tent after supper.

"I don't want to live here forever," he said. "Did you look and see if the ring gear came today?"

"I forgot," I said.

"But you were right in Germfask," he said. "Why didn't you look?"

"I told you. I forgot."

"You were probably monkeying around with that Jean MacKenzie."

"God," I said, "I forgot her, too."

FOURTEEN

There were good days and bad days. On that Wednesday evening I had experienced three what I would call good days in a row. I was about to have a bad one. George had come down to the tent that night to bring some groceries he'd taken from one of the cabins. There were quite a few odds and ends and after he'd gone up to the big house I sorted them out and took the food over to the icehouse where it would be safe from marauding animals. There was one item that I left sitting on the picnic table, however. It was a box of soap chips. It was still sitting there when I crawled in the tent and went to sleep that night.

Almost from the time we'd arrived in Charlie Fuller's camp, we'd had dogs nosing around our tent. Two of them belonged to Charlie and the others belonged to one or another of the campers. All of them were friendly enough and neither George nor I had experienced any trouble with them. We'd learned to take them for granted. Ever since my run-in with the bear, I'd always been careful to keep a big pile of firewood close to the entrance to the tent. Quite often, if I woke up in the night, I would reach out and throw a few sticks on the dying fire. On the night after I sold Charlie the

Monkey Tire Patch, I woke up around three o'clock and sleepily reached for the wood. To my surprise, when I looked out, I saw a big dog with his forepaws up on the picnic table. He was obviously eating something. I quickly threw three sticks on the fire and reached for another one and threw it at the dog, yelling, "Get out of here!" at the top of my voice. He turned his head and looked at me and I saw the skin draw back on his upper lip to reveal the nastiest set of fangs I ever saw. To make matters worse, he seemed to be frothing at the mouth. For a few seconds I was thoroughly frightened and then I realized that the reason he was frothing at the mouth was because he'd been trying to eat those soap chips. I relaxed. The dog didn't. He continued to stand there and a menacing snarl reached my ears. The wood that I had thrown on the fire burst into bright flame and when the dog didn't move I reached out and grabbed up one of the flaming brands and tossed it at the dog's feet. With a truly ferocious growl his feet came down off that bench and he started straight at me. I thought he was going to leap, but if he had done so he would have had to jump straight across the fire. He stopped and looked at me and growled and backed off. In doing so his hind foot stepped squarely on that flaming stick I had thrown at him. He yelped and jumped and whirled to face the stick and I think he may have stuck his nose too close to it. At any rate, he let out another yelp and put his tail between his legs and slunk out into the woods. In almost the same situation, the bear had disappeared completely, but the dog didn't. For the next half hour I could hear him off in the fringe of the woods and every now and then I caught the sound of that snarl. Once I thought I heard two dogs out there. I kept a club beside me, but eventually I went back to sleep.

One never slept very late in that tent and I was up and about before five o'clock. My first chore of the day was to build up the campfire and the second one was to take a pail and go over to the spring behind the barn for water.

On the way over there I bumped into Charlie loping along at his habitual dogtrot on his way up from the barn.

"Say, Charlie," I said to him, "if you see one of the camper's dogs running around with foam coming out of his mouth, don't worry about it. He's not mad. He was down at my tent in the middle of the night eating soap chips."

"What kind of a dog was it?"

"I don't know. A mongrel of some kind. Gray colored and very big. I guess it was some kind of a police dog only it had a broader nose."

"I don't remember any dog like that around here," Charlie said, and then frowned. "What color did you say it was?"

"Gray. Maybe it belonged to MacKenzie."

"MacKenzie has a setter bitch and it knows better than to come on my property. Did you say that dog was big?"

"Yes."

"And mean-looking?"

"Meanest-looking dog I ever saw."

Charlie nodded. "All alone?"

"It's funny you'd say that. I only saw one, but I would have sworn I heard another one in the woods."

Charlie pursed his lips. "Son, that wasn't no dog. That was a timber wolf. They come around here once in a while. I hope you didn't try to pick a fight."

"I threw a stick at him."

"You're lucky you're still alive." He shook his head. "If he was eating soap chips, he was hungry. You run on down to the barn for me and tell George not to take those cattle out to pasture for a while."

By the time I told George and got my pail of water and started back to the tent, I met Charlie coming down the path. He was carrying three rifles and Mr. Jackson was with him, still half asleep, carrying another one.

"Put down that pail, boy," Charlie said, and thrust a rifle at me. "We're going wolf hunting. Those varmints won't go very far away from here if they are hungry and if they get the scent of those cattle."

I put down the pail and followed along behind the others. Charlie gave George the other rifle and then led the way out into the woods. We spent the next four hours wandering around in that underbrush. I didn't see a thing. Neither did George, but just before the end Charlie brought up his rifle and I heard a shot. It was followed quickly by another shot from Mr. Jackson's gun.

"I think I got him," Charlie said. "How about you, Jackson?"

"I don't think I hit him," Mr. Jackson said.

"I thought you were a better shot than that, Jackson," Charlie said.

"I'll get him next time," Mr. Jackson said.

"There won't be no next time. Right now those two wolves are clear over in Schoolcraft County and running hard. They know better than to stay around here after that."

"I thought you said you hit yours," Mr. Jackson said.

"Oh, I hit him all right, but I don't know where I hit him. Probably in the shoulder. Not enough to stop him. Anyway, he won't be bothering us any more." He turned to George. "You can let those cattle out now."

That wolf hunt took so long that I didn't get to go into Germfask that day. I was also late getting my batch of muffins up to the kitchen for Mrs. Fuller.

"If you're going to keep on being late with these things, I'm going to cancel my order," she said.

"I don't think that's very fair, Mrs. Fuller," I said. "I was out protecting you and your daughters from wolves."

"You didn't do much protecting the way I hear it. Charlie said you never even saw them and they were almost under your feet."

"I know, but I tried."

She walked across the kitchen and took a close look at me. "You have any of that poison ivy stuff left?"

180

"A little," I said.

"Well, you'd better use it. You must have got in a big patch of it."

She was right. I began to itch almost at once. I went back down to the tent and got out the bottle and spread the stuff all over me. After I'd finished, I got out George's bottle of purple ointment and went looking for him.

"How did you know?" he said.

"Mrs. Fuller told me. Put it on there before you have to go see the doctor again."

It wasn't until after George had finished that I thought of Mr. Jackson. I took both bottles of ointment up to him at the house.

"You'd better try both of them," I said. "You never know which is going to work."

The white fluid did the job for him and after he was finished applying it, he thanked me.

"If you hadn't come around with that, I'd have had to go all the way to Newberry," he said.

"Only to Curtis. There's a poison ivy specialist over there. Also Finns and Indians and butchers. They all dance together on Saturday nights."

"I know. I went once. Those dances are square dances. You can have them. By the way, speaking of dances, have you ever found that girl of yours over at Germfask?"

"I've seen her," I said, "but I haven't talked with her."

"Well, Mrs. Jackson and I are going home on Sunday. We thought we'd celebrate Saturday night by going down to Blaney. Why don't you get hold of that girl and come along with us?"

"I can't," I said. "Mrs. Fuller won't let me use the phone."

"Why on earth not?"

"Because that girl's name is Jean MacKenzie and you're not supposed to call anybody named MacKenzie from this house."

He nodded. "I understand," he said. "I'll drive you in tomorrow afternoon."

"I wouldn't want you to do that," I said. "This is your last two days here. You probably want to go fishing."

"As a matter of fact, I do," he said. "But you take the car and drive in yourself. My wife is going shopping over at the Indian reservation in the morning. She'll be back around one o'clock."

I couldn't have arranged it better if I'd planned it. I came driving up to MacKenzie's house about three o'clock the next afternoon and went up and knocked on the door. Jean answered it.

"Well," she said, "where have you been? I thought you'd left the country."

"Oh, I had a few chores to take care of last week, but now I'm ready for action. I thought we might try something non-athletic. Like dancing maybe."

"When?"

"Tomorrow night, down at Blaney."

"Oh, that's too bad," she said. "Tomorrow's the last day of the golf tournament and I expect to win it. They give the winner a dinner party. I have to go."

"Well, we could dance after the dinner." I carefully stood aside so that she could get a good look at the LaSalle.

She considered it, and then she considered me. "Well," she said, "I think that would be nice. The trouble is that it might be late before the dinner is over with."

"That won't make any difference, except for one thing." I shook my head as though I was worried. "I was going to go with a friend of mine and his girl. They want to get there early. I suppose I could let him take the car and go on ahead. Do you suppose you could pick me up after your dinner is over with?"

"Sure," she said. "I'll have my car with me anyway. I'll meet you at about nine-thirty. But you'll have to come down to the corner where the CC road cuts off. My grandfather won't let me set foot on Charlie Fuller's property."

"That's all right with me," I said. "I'll see you at nine-thirty tomorrow night."

She waved at me as I bounced down the steps and got in the car. She was still standing there in the doorway when I last saw her. That little thing had gone so well that I was almost sure everything would turn for the better. I went to the post office, fully expecting to find the ring gear. I didn't, but I did find a letter for George. It was the very first mail that we had received from home and we'd now been gone for almost four weeks. This letter, I knew, was good news because it had George's mother's return address in the upper left-hand corner.

The minute I got back to the camp and turned the car over to Mr. Jackson, I went looking for George. I found him down at the dock with Charlie. They were just getting in the boat to go up the lake seining for minnows. I ran out onto the dock waving the letter in the air so that George could see it and he stood up in the boat and held out his hand for it. He was just about to tear it open when Charlie barked at him to pay attention to business and cast off the line that held the boat to the dock. George quickly stuffed the envelope in his back pocket and shoved off as Charlie started the outboard motor.

Seining for minnows with Charlie Fuller was no picnic as I well knew. On these expeditions, usually way up at the other end of the lake, Charlie carried a metal, fifty-five-gallon drum half full of water. This sat on a couple of boards that had been placed from gunwale to gunwale amidships of the boat. When Charlie reached the place where he wanted to cast his net the helper in the bow would stand up and take one end of the seine and help with the cast. Then the two men would pull it in, hand over hand. When it was finally lifted out of the water it might contain two hundred pounds of struggling minnows. These had to be lifted laboriously and bodily out of the water and dumped from the net into the barrel. It was an awkward job because both men were working in a confined space on relatively unsteady footing. When the men lifted all that weight out of the water there were three or four minutes of good hard labor. Charlie usually made three casts on each of these seining trips and in between casts he would usually rest for five minutes. It was practically the only time I ever saw him rest.

It was during the first rest period that George remembered the envelope I had handed him. He reached around and pulled it out of his back pocket and tore it open. As he did so a piece of blue paper came fluttering out and the wind caught it and wafted it out over the lake where it slowly settled to the surface of the water. For some reason George didn't notice this piece of paper. I suppose he thought it was the lining out of the envelope that he had torn rather roughly. But when he read the first two lines he looked up. His mother had told him that she was enclosing a postal money order for ten dollars. George looked in the envelope and it wasn't there. Then he looked down at the bottom of the boat to see if it had dropped out. It was about then that he remembered the piece of blue paper. He twisted around frantically and looked out over the lake. There, on the surface of the water about twenty feet away, was the precious money order. George didn't hesitate. He stood up and dived, clothes, shoes, and all. He reached the money order, grasped it in his hand, held it high in the air, and paddled back to the boat. He tried to climb in over the bow, but it was too high for him to reach so he paddled back to the stern and held up his hand for Charlie to give him a pull. This might have worked under ordinary circumstances, but with that barrel of minnows sitting amidships the boat was top heavy. Instead of George coming up, the boat capsized. Charlie, the barrel of minnows, the net, and all the rest of the gear ended up in Big Manistique Lake. Evidently

Charlie had been through shipwrecks like this before because he knew just what to do. He saved the barrel from sinking, got the net fastened to it, and lashed the outboard motor to the stern so that it wouldn't be lost. Then he got the boat righted, climbed back into it and pulled George in. After that the two went to work salvaging all the equipment. When they got it all back in place, they went back to seining. Unfortunately, the motor was wet and wouldn't start so they had to row all the way home, a distance of about eight miles. They didn't get back to the camp until almost dark.

That was the end of George as far as Charlie was concerned. He came stalking down to the tent about ten o'clock and told me to move up to the big house on Saturday afternoon. He'd fired George, effective when the week's work was done. I didn't see George, himself, until the next morning when he caught me on the way back from my daily visit to the cove. He didn't seem to be bothered at all about losing his job. He pulled the money order from his pocket and handed it to me.

"Are you going into Germfask today?" he asked.

"I hadn't planned on it. Why?"

"I wish you would. I'd like you to cash that money order for me so I can use it tonight."

I looked at it absent-mindedly and then looked at George.

"Jesus, George, nobody will cash this."

"Why not?" he said belligerently.

"Because nobody can tell how much it's for. All the ink has run together in one big blob."

"I know how much it's for," he said. "It's for ten dollars. It says so right here in this letter my mother sent me."

"That's not going to do you any good. That lady in the Germfask post office isn't going to take your word for it, or your mother's word, either."

"You mean the whole ten dollars is shot?"

"No. I don't think it's shot. Your mother has the receipt

for it. When you get home you can take the money order and the receipt down to the post office and they'll probably cash it."

"I don't want the money when I get home. I want it right now, while I'm up here. I want it for tonight."

"You don't need it for tonight. You got money left over from guiding last Sunday and you get paid this afternoon."

"I know all that, but I want it tonight. I want to buy a bottle of booze. I think I can get someplace with that girl if I can get a drink into her."

"Haven't you got anyplace with her yet?"

"No. It's hard work."

"I should think it would be. You're going about it the wrong way. Whoever heard of getting anyplace with a girl at a square dance or on a park bench in the middle of town?"

"I didn't ask for any advice. All I want to know is if you're going to take it to Germfask and get it cashed for me."

"No," I said.

"You're a fine friend, you are."

"Maybe next week, when you're not working, you'll go in once in a while and see if that ring gear has come."

FIFTEEN

At the moment George stopped me and asked me to go to Germfask for him, I wasn't in any mood to do anything for anyone. I had just seen Jean MacKenzie take her usual dip in the lake and I had only one thing on my mind—sex. The culmination of all those weeks of watching was at hand. This was the day I was going to have my date with this magnificent specimen of womanhood. It never entered my mind that it wouldn't come out the way I anticipated it. The entire fortune at my disposal would be dedicated to the proposition. I had eleven dollars now. That would be enough to buy a few drinks. There would be an evening of dancing to the soft strains of romantic music while I got the drinks into Jean and then, at dawn, we would quietly retire to the cove and have a swimming party.

I didn't leave anything to chance. When I made up my daily batch of muffins and took it up to Mrs. Fuller at the big house, I asked her for permission to use her flat iron. She gave me the permission—in return for one free batch of muffins. I dug my one good pair of pants out of my suitcase in the back of the car and carefully pressed them. I ironed my good shirt. I scrubbed all my dirty underwear and hung it out in the sun to dry. I took a spot off my neck-tie. By three in the afternoon I was ready to go as far as my basic equipment was concerned. At that point I had another piece of luck. Mr. Jackson came to me and informed me that he'd like to take a mess of fish home with him. He wanted to be sure he caught some and so he had asked Charlie to guide him. Charlie already had a fishing party and couldn't accommodate him and recommended me. Mr. Jackson was willing to pay me two dollars for three hours of my time. I still didn't know anything about where to catch fish, but I remembered that day when the pike were practically jumping in my boat.

Charlie was no dummy. He knew what I knew and he knew how to get around it. He left a little note in the boat-house telling me to look around the lake until I spotted a yellow boat. That would be him. If I went a half mile east of there I would catch fish. I did exactly as I was told and I caught fish. As a matter of fact, between us Mr. Jackson and I caught twenty-five of them. Mr. Jackson was enthu-siastic and wanted to pay me three dollars, but I wouldn't take it. I told him if he was really grateful he could buy my girl and me a drink when we got down to Blaney. I was making sure Jean got good and loaded.

When I got back from the fishing I found George all dressed and ready to go to Curtis. He was still angry with me for not going into Germfask. When he stomped out of my sight he informed me that he might not be back for two or three days. I couldn't have cared less. I moved all my belongings up to the little room in the basement of the big house. As a matter of fact I moved more than I ordinarily would have because I expected that this time I would be making a long stay. When I got up to the big house with all my things I was disgusted to find that George hadn't moved out. All his work clothes and his suitcase were strewn around the room where he had left them. I just picked up everything and made a bundle out of it and went down and threw it in the tent. After that I took a shower and got all dressed up. By the time I finished preening it was past eight o'clock. Jingling my money in my pocket and my rosy dreams in my head, I sauntered down the road out of Charlie's place, came eventually to the corner where the CCC road turned off, and took up a waiting position on my rock.

I arrived at that rock around quarter of nine. Nine o'clock came, then nine-fifteen, and finally nine-thirty. There were no cars traveling in either direction. The night was absolutely black. I began to think about the wolves and the bear and I began to look around me uneasily. Ten o'clock arrived and departed. At ten-thirty I stopped worrying about wild animals and began worrying about Jean MacKenzie. At eleven o'clock I looked at my watch and told myself I would give her fifteen more minutes. Promptly at eleven-fifteen I saw a pair of headlights speeding down the road from the direction of Germfask. They came straight at me and the car slid to a stop not ten feet away from me. To my great surprise I recognized Mr. Jackson's LaSalle. I went around to the driver's side and looked in. There was Jean Mac-Kenzie smiling up at me in a beatific fashion. Beside her on the front seat and stuffed at various angles in the rumble seat were what looked like a horde of people.

"I knew you wouldn' mind 'f I borrowed y'r car," Jean said. "Been wantin' to drive it so when I saw it in the parkin' lot, I thought it would be a good chance."

I stood there, horror-struck. Not only had she stolen Mr. Jackson's car, but she was quite drunk. I looked back up the road to Germfask wondering how many times she had run in and out of ditches.

"Some car," she said. "I got it up to eighty once on the way up from Blaney."

I opened the door. "Move over," I said. "I'll drive."

"You're not mad at me, are you?" she said. "I'm just doin'

a li'l celebratin'. You're ridin' with the new woman's golf champion from Blaney Lodge."

I backed the car around and headed it back toward Germfask.

"I'm not mad," I said. "I'm just scared."

"What're you scared of? Little old me?" She reached over and gave me a big wet kiss on the side of the mouth. "Well, all I c'n say is, you needn' be." She turned around and began tossing off a string of names in what I took to be a series of introductions.

"I'm not scared of you," I said. "I'm thinking about Mr. Jackson."

"Who's Mr. Jackson?" she asked.

"I have a feeling you'll find out any minute now." I pressed grimly ahead, keeping the speed down to twenty miles an hour, just hoping that I'd get back to Blaney safely. Jean MacKenzie looked up at me uncertainly and then turned back to the others.

"What this big he-man needs is a li'l drink," she said. "Pass that bottle up here."

The next thing I knew I found a half-full bottle of whiskey thrust in front of my eyes. I was faced with an extremely important decision. I was driving a stolen car already. If I took a drink out of the bottle, I might also be making myself eligible for arrest as a drunken driver. On the other hand I'd been building up to this date all summer and I sensed that if I didn't take a drink I might lose this girl before I even got started. Besides that, I had to get the bottle out from in front of my eyes so I could see to do the driving. I stopped the car and grabbed the bottle and took a small swig. Then I handed it back to Jean.

"Aha!" she said. "Now the party will liven up."

It didn't need livening up. I never did know just how many people were stuffed in that car, but I think there were three other couples besides Jean and myself. I think there were two couples in the rumble seat and I kept hearing one girl say over and over, "I told you now, get your god-damned hand off my leg or I'll bust you one." One of the fellows back there was singing in his girl's ear. He wasn't a very good singer and he wasn't singing a very good song. Over on the other side of the car's front seat there seemed to be a tangle of arms and legs, but I couldn't see who they belonged to. Every now and then I would hear a girl let loose a loud and coarse burst of laughter so I assumed at least one person was whispering dirty jokes in her ear.

That was a nightmarish ride. I always have a feeling that at some point I was standing off by the side of the road and watching that car go by full of waving arms and legs and whiskey bottles. I'm quite sure that if we'd passed anyone they would have had us arrested on general principles. I was detached from the whole thing, of course. I was sober and they were all quite drunk. I didn't know how many of them there were and I didn't know who they were or what their names were. About all I knew was that every now and then the whiskey bottle would pop up in front of my eyes as we ambled along the road and I would stop the car and take a little taste and hand the bottle back to Jean. That was the only time she seemed to pay any attention to me—when she passed that bottle. The rest of the time she was turned around talking to the others. She may have been the one who was listening to the dirty jokes. I couldn't tell.

After what seemed like an endless journey I saw the blaze of lights from the clubhouse at Blaney Lodge and I wheeled into the driveway and glided to a stop in the parking lot. The minute I shut the engine off, the bottle began its last round. As each person finished his drink, he or she would unwind and climb out of the car and wander off. I was the very last one to get the bottle. When I tipped it up I found there were only two or three drops left. When I put it down, I found I was alone. Jean was just disappearing. She had slid across the seat and let herself out the door and was now skipping gaily down the golf course. I climbed out and tried to follow her, but she had on a dark dress and I soon lost sight of her in the darkness. After I got about one hundred yards down the fairway I came to a stand of small trees. I went over and looked into it uncertainly. I couldn't see anyone and I couldn't hear anyone. I called Jean's name twice, but there was no answer. I decided that there was only one sensible thing to do and that was to go back to the clubhouse. Sooner or later Jean would be bound to show up there. I was quite sure I'd be able to recognize her despite the fact that she wasn't wearing jodhpurs, a one-piece bathing suit, or the altogether. On the way back to the clubhouse I did have presence of mind enough to roll up all the windows in Mr. Jackson's car, lock the doors, and take the keys out of the ignition.

Blaney Lodge was a fine spacious place and this was the first time I had seen it. I had remembered to bring along the guest card I'd received from Charlie Fuller and I presented it at the door. I was directed into what must have been the main dining room, but the tables had all been moved back from the center to uncover a fairly large dance floor. There must have been a hundred people in the place, probably the upper crust of all that part of the upper peninsula. Most of the men were dressed in summer suits and the women all had on long dresses. The Jacksons had a table about halfway up one wall of the room and two other couples were seated with them. It was an intermission of some kind and they were all sipping drinks. When I came up the men all got to their feet and I was introduced to everyone. After I sat down and ordered a drink, I shoved the car keys over to Mr. Jackson. He raised his eyebrows.

"When I came through the parking lot just now, I found some people necking in your car," I lied. "I locked it up."

"I know, but no one ever locks their car in the upper peninsula," Mr. Jackson said.

"They'd better begin," I said.

When the music started to play I danced with Mrs. Jackson and then I took a turn with the other two ladies. I forgot all about Jean MacKenzie. It must have been well on toward one o'clock when she showed up. I was just walking off the dance floor when I felt a tug at my sleeve. I turned to find Jean standing at my elbow. When I'd last seen her she had been skipping along the fairway, feeling no pain. Now she was quite drunk. Her hair was in disarray and her dress was mussed up and she was decidedly unsteady on her feet.

"Where have you been?" she asked me querulously.

"I've been right here all the time. Where have you been?"

"Out playin' golf, natcherly." She giggled.

"I thought this was supposed to be a non-athletic date."

A drunken smile crossed her face. "That's a pretty good joke," she said. She shook her head. "A very funny joke." Just at that moment the orchestra began to play. She shook her finger at me. "I wanna dance," she said. "You gonna dance with me?"

I steered her out onto the dance floor and took her in my arms. If she had been sober I think she would have been a fine dancer. There was something quite strong and graceful about her, but in her present condition she leaned heavily on me and stumbled a good deal. I think we danced about one number before she pushed me away.

"You got to tell me about yourself," she said. "I don't know nothing about you. I gotta find out."

"Where do you want me to start?" I asked.

She looked around. "This ain't no place to talk," she said. "Let's get out of here. All right with you?"

I nodded and she took my hand and led me out through a side door and pulled me along toward the parking lot. We came to her little roadster and she opened the door and climbed in and slid part way across the seat, then beckoned to me. When I sat down behind the driver's wheel, she slid over against me.

"Now put your arms around me and don't ask for no more instructions."

I did as I was told. We were still in the midst of our first torrid kiss and things had already taken a turn in the direction I intended when I heard a voice, almost in my ear.

"Hey, Jean," it said. "What're you doing?"

She straightened up and turned around and glared at the intruder. "What the hell does it look like I'm doing?" she said. "I'm neckin', that's what I'm doin'. What's the idea of snoopin' around here just when things are gettin' interestin'?"

"Caroline's passed out," the boy whined. "You gotta do something. Her mother'll kill me."

"Oh, God! All right! All right!" Jean slid across the seat to the other side of the car and kicked the door open and stumbled off down the golf course in the dark. I jumped out of my side and ran around to follow her, but she stopped and pointed a finger at me.

"You stay right there. This girl's not in any shape to be seen by any stranger. I'll be back in five minutes."

She wasn't back in five minutes. She wasn't back in ten minutes. At the end of half an hour, I set out to try and find her. I must have walked halfway around that golf course before I gave up. I slowly made my way back to the clubhouse. To my horror I found the lights turned out and the parking lot empty. Not only Jean's car was gone, but so was the Jacksons'. I went over to the road and started walking. By daylight I was just coming down the hill into Germfask. By ten o'clock I was just stumbling up the hill into Charlie Fuller's camp. I was so tired I even forgot I was supposed to be sleeping up at the big house. I just crawled into the tent and went to bed.

SIXTEEN

I had no trouble erasing Jean MacKenzie from my
mind. I was working for Charlie Fuller. It wasn't even
necessary to throw myself into my work. Charlie threw me
into it. I spent three cheerless days dog trotting back and
forth with fifty-pound chunks of ice, armloads of wood,
and thirty-gallon milk cans. There wasn't much to cheer
me up, either. The Jacksons' departure had taken place
before I climbed out of the tent on Sunday afternoon.
George was nowhere in evidence. I went down to our
camp three nights running and the place was dull and life-
less and unlived in.

It was on Thursday night when George came dragging
into my basement room. He had a black eye and he was in
an ugly mood.

"Where did you put my things?" he asked me.

"I took them down and put them in the tent," I said. "You
didn't think I was going to step over them every time I came
in here, did you?"

"By God, that money order better not be lost."

"Didn't you take it with you? Where did you leave it?"

"It was in the pocket of my work pants. I forgot it."

"Then it's still in the pocket of your work pants. I didn't touch it and nobody's been down there." He turned to go. "Where did you get that black eye?" I said.

"My girl's brother gave it to me."

"Boy, you must have got someplace."

"No, I didn't get anyplace, but I will now."

"What makes you think so?"

"I told them I'm a Norwegian. That practically makes me one of the family."

Shortly after that Charlie came down and sent me off to the icehouse to bring up ice for a cabin we were opening up to have ready for any late arrivals. I happened to remember that I had cleaned out some groceries the day before so I went over to our tent to tell George. He'd started the fires and smudges by then.

"George, there's a slice of ham and a dozen eggs over in the hiding place. I got them out of Cabin One yesterday morning. I thought you might like a good breakfast in the morning. It's all yours."

He looked up at me sheepishly. "Gee, thanks. I'm sorry I got sore at you."

"That's all right," I said. "Did you find the money order?"

"Yeah. It was in my pocket, right where I left it. I think I'll go into Germfask early in the morning and see if I can cash it. I can use the money. I'm broke."

I didn't see him at all the next day. As Mrs. Fuller said, Charlie's camp was full up. There just wasn't time enough to do all the work. On that particular night, a Friday, Charlie and I went out seining for minnows at the other end of the lake. We didn't even leave the dock until it was getting dark and we didn't get home until after ten. Just before I went to bed, after midnight, I looked down at the tent to see if George was back yet. The fires were out so I knew he wasn't there. Remembering all the run-ins I'd had with wildlife, I had half a notion to run down there and build a fire. It was a good thing I didn't.

Ever since my experience with the porcupine and the bear, I'd been very scrupulous about not leaving any food around the tent. I'd been careful to impress this rule on George, too. That was why we took all our grocery hauls over to the icehouse whenever we found them. On that morning after he came back from Curtis, George had gone over to our cache and got the ham and the dozen eggs. He'd fried three of the eggs for breakfast and then, because he was in such a hurry to get to Germfask to cash his money order, he'd gotten careless. He'd just shoved the rest of the eggs in the tent and had gone on his merry way. I'd been right about the money order. The postmistress in Germfask had refused to cash it. George had argued with her for an hour or more and then he decided to try the post office in Curtis. It had taken him a considerable amount of time to walk into Germfask and it took him even longer to walk and hitchhike the seventeen miles back to Curtis. By the time he finished arguing unsuccessfully with the Curtis postmaster, it was suppertime and so he dropped around to cadge a meal from his new-found relatives. As a result it was after three o'clock in the morning—Saturday—when he got home. He was so tired with all that walking and arguing and whatever it was he did on the town bench in Curtis that he didn't even bother to build up the fires. He just took off his shoes and climbed in between his blankets. Porcupines can be painful, bears can be frightening, and wolves can be dangerous, but any way one looks at it, skunks are impossible. When George crawled in the tent that night he laid down right beside a skunk who was peacefully making a meal out of those leftover eggs. The skunk showed his displeasure in the only way skunks have. When George discovered the enormity of his situation he let out a howl that could be heard all the way to Germfask. It certainly didn't take the rest of us in Charlie's camp very long to realize that there was no wolf down there with him.

George had all the right instincts. With the first pop of the gun, so to speak, he was off and running. He didn't stop running until he got to Jean MacKenzie's cove. Arrived there, he dived in the water head first with all his clothes on. He was still standing there in the water up to his neck when Jean came for her dip three hours later. She smelled him first, and then she saw him. Quite naturally, she didn't go swimming that morning, nor did she go swimming at all for a week.

That Saturday must have been the worst day Charlie Fuller's camp ever had. The skunk scent hung over everything. One not only inhaled it with his breath, but it seemed to permeate clothes and the food one ate. The exodus began at dawn as fishermen suddenly decided to go trout fishing at Taquahmenon River, thirty miles away. Golfers went for an early round at Blaney Park. Sightseers moved up their trip to the Soo Locks. About halfway through the forenoon Charlie climbed in his old truck with his wife, daughters, and mother-in-law and drove over to Manistique to take care of some business or other. I was told that this was the first time he had been absent from his camp in the summertime since he built it. I was caught, of course. I had to walk around in the stink all day long doing the necessary chores. Since Charlie wasn't around to supervise and since the camp was utterly deserted, I had virtually nothing to do, but I didn't enjoy it. Several times, from a safe distance, I shouted instructions to George about what to do. I managed to talk him out of the water around noon. He emerged half frozen and buried all his clothes. (One of the great tragedies was the fact that he buried the money order with the clothes and I could never get him to dig it up.) With much prodding I also managed to get him to bury our tent and everything that was in it. It was all ruined beyond redemption and that included every stitch of clothing George owned, for I had thrown the whole works in the tent on the previous Saturday when I took over the chores. I got together some underwear and my extra pants and shirt for George to wear, but I didn't have any shoes that would fit him so he had to go around barefoot. Fortunately, for us, we had one extra pup tent still stashed away in the back of the car and it had escaped damage. When it finally came time to use it, I borrowed two blankets from a friendly camper, but that wasn't for two days. It was simply impossible for anyone to live down there in that old camp until the smell began to peter out. Needless to say, George was treated like a leper for some little time. Even I didn't like to go near him. For two nights, after every one in the camp had gone to bed and the lights were turned out, George would sneak up onto the front porch of the big house and curl up and try to sleep. He was a pathetic figure.

It was on Monday night, just as the skunk crisis was beginning to subside, that we had our last disaster. Early in the evening Charlie had taken a fishing party out on the lake. He had instructed me, among other things, to sweep out the boathouse while he was gone. I was in the midst of this when I detected George's now familiar odor coming down the stairs from the bluff. He stuck his head in the door, a forlorn figure, and asked me if he could have a few serious words with me.

"You have to do me a favor," he said. "I don't have a cent of money, but I've got to have some shoes and socks. I don't want to borrow any money, you understand, but I do want you to do something for me."

"What?" I said.

He pointed at the slot machine. "Do you suppose we could hit that jackpot again?"

"Sure," I said. "Why not?"

I went over to Charlie's toolbox and got out his screwdriver and George went to work. When he had everything set, he put the cover back in place and I slipped the first nickel in the slot. I think it took us eight or ten plays to get the jackpot. I shoved the money at George.

"No," he said. "Split it up."

"I don't need it, George. You do. You can't get much of a pair of shoes with half of it."

"I can get a pair of sneakers for a dollar and a quarter. That's all I need."

I argued with him for about five minutes and he wouldn't take the money so I split it up. Each of us netted a dollar and thirty-five cents. George took his money and disappeared. I put a handful of nickels in my pocket and went back to sweeping the floor. After I finished I put my broom away and locked up the boathouse and went on to do my next chore. We'd made one big mistake. In the course of arguing about splitting up the money, George had forgotten to take the back off the machine and set it the way Charlie had left it. About an hour later Charlie and his fishing party came back to the dock. The first thing one of the fishermen did was to put a nickel in the machine. Three plums came up. The machine should have paid off twelve nickels, but with Charlie and George and I milking it the way we had, there weren't that many nickels left in the pay-off tube. Only six came out. The fisherman complained, naturally, and Charlie had to make up the deficit out of his pocket. The man put one of his nickels in to take off the plums and three oranges came up. Instead of eight nickels, only one dropped down and once again Charlie had to make up the difference. That was too much for him. He immediately scribbled out a big sign that said "Out of order" and put it on the machine. After the fisherman had gone, Charlie got out his screwdriver and looked to see what was making the machine pay off so often. He discovered the setting change immediately and it wasn't hard for him to guess who the culprits were. He came storming up to the house where I was washing up for supper.

"Boy," he said, pointing his finger at me, "you're fired! You and your good-for-nothing skunky friend get off this property. I'll give you one hour."

"Not so fast," I said. "Our rent is paid up until Wednesday

morning at ten o'clock. Either give me back the rent that's not used up, or we stay until Wednesday."

I knew that Charlie would never give back a penny once he got his hands on it. "All right," he said. "Wednesday morning at ten o'clock."

"Your wife owes me fifty cents for two batches of muffins. Do you want to pay me that, or do you want to let us stay an extra two days and a half?"

"Two days and eight hours," he said. "I want you off the property by Friday night at six o'clock. Now take your stuff and get back down to your tent where you belong."

"Wait a minute," I said. "I've put in a full day's work. I'm entitled to supper."

"Take the money you got out of that slot machine and buy yourself some supper," he said, and turned around and stalked out of the room.

We were all but done in Charlie's camp and I knew it.

SEVENTEEN

George and I had quite an important conference over our campfire that night. I told him that we had to move by Friday, no matter what. The big problem was the car. Either he had to make up his mind to abandon it or else he had to save it. It was up to him and whatever was done he would have to do.

"I don't think that's fair," he said. "You promised it to me after this trip was over and I think you ought to keep your promise."

"I don't care whether it's fair or not. I can't help it."

"Well, there's a guy over in Curtis that goes to all the dances. He works in a gas station and his boss has a truck. I think maybe I could talk him into coming over and towing us to MacKenzie's camp."

"You mean to sit there and tell me that you've known a guy with a tow truck all along and you've sat here and let us work our ass off for Charlie?"

"I didn't know him all along. I didn't meet him until last week. After he found out I was a Norwegian he came around and introduced himself. He said he was Norwegian, too, and that he was tired of talking to nobody but Finns."

"Well, I guess that black eye was worth something," I said. "You go over there tomorrow and get him and his truck over here. I'll rig up a Norwegian flag for you to wave if I have to."

"I can't," he said.

"Why not?"

"I have to wait for this skunk smell to wear off a little bit. Give me another day. I'll tell you what. You go over to Germfask tomorrow and see if that ring gear has come yet. If it has, I'll fix this and we'll get out of here. If it hasn't come yet, I'll go over to Curtis and get the tow truck."

I got up early the next morning and walked into Germfask. There was no ring gear in the post office, but Jean MacKenzie was there. She walked out the front door with me.

"I'm sorry about the other night," she said. "I didn't act very nicely, did I?"

"Well, I guess it isn't every day you get to be the woman's golf champion of Blaney Park."

"I'd really like to make it up to you some way." She seemed very contrite. "Would you like to try it again?"

"No more dances for me," I said. "I'm afraid I'm no social lion."

"How about the swimming part? It's going to be moonlight this week. We could have a swimming party."

"Would that same gang be there?"

"Some of them, I guess."

"No thanks," I said.

She sighed. "You really think I'm horrible, don't you? Well, I don't guess I blame you."

It's a funny thing about girls. I think that most of the time they can wrap a man around their little finger with no trouble at all. For almost six weeks I had been thinking fond, if lascivious, thoughts about Jean MacKenzie and for most of those weeks she hadn't even noticed me. Now the situation was reversed. My eyes had been opened. If she'd ever had any glamour at all, that night at the Blaney Lodge had stripped it all away. Instead of the picture of a magnificent female body—the image that I had been carrying so long—I now carried around in my mind a picture of a coarse, sloppy, drunken girl who repelled me rather than attracted me. Nothing that had happened in the post office had changed any of that. I was still indifferent when I opened the door of her car for her to let her in, but when I looked down at her, I looked right in her eyes. The message in them said everything that she couldn't put into words. She was saying, "I'm not so bad. Give me a chance to show you. You'll like me." The words she actually used were different, of course.

"Are you out walking again?"

"Yes."

"Well, get in. I'll give you a ride home."

I went around and opened the door and slid into the seat without saying a word. She made a U-turn, reached the corner by the CCC barracks, and ducked into the road that led out to Charlie's camp. She drove quietly for a half mile, until we passed over a slight hill that shut Germfask off from our view. Then she pulled over to the side of the narrow road and stopped the car and shut off the motor. The next thing she was in my arms and I was kissing her passionately. Jean MacKenzie was the kind of a girl who aroused a man and she, herself, was easily aroused. There was no question in my mind about what she wanted from me. I wanted it as much as she did and I didn't intend to dally about it. We spent five of the more sensuous moments in history and then we were interrupted. I must have walked into Germfask and back fifteen times in those weeks I was at Charlie's camp and on the majority of those walks I'd never seen a car on that road. Now, for some reason or other, every one in the upper peninsula seemed to have decided to make the trip between Germfask and Curtis. Jean and I were wrapped together, oblivious to the world, when there was a loud and raucous blast of a horn behind us. Jean struggled to sit up and turned to look at the car that had drawn up behind us. She pulled down her skirt and slid over behind the wheel and started the motor. We moved along until we came to a wide spot in the road and she pulled over and motioned for the car to go by. As it passed we could see a whole family of necks and eyes turned our way. As the car rolled on, the rear window filled up with these same necks and eyes. The car went down the road for half a mile, now rolling so slowly that I thought it would stop any moment. Jean shook her head and bit her lip and shifted gears. We pulled out of the wide spot and began to pick up speed. The car in front spurted ahead in a cloud of dust and was soon only a speck in the distance. Jean slowed to a stop and turned off the motor and came over to me. Once more we worked ourselves into a passion. This time we reached the gasping and moaning stage and then there was that familiar honk of a horn behind us. We went through almost exactly the same performance as before. Three times that afternoon we almost reached the point of consummation and three times we had to stop. Three quarters of an hour after we left Germfask we reached the road that led off across the swamp and she stopped the car.

"This certainly isn't any good," she said. "I think we'd better have that swimming party, all by ourselves."

"I'd enjoy that," I said. "When? Tonight?"

"No. I can't. I'm going to be in a wedding tomorrow night and I have to go to rehearsal tonight. It will have to be Thursday."

"Thursday?"

"Yes. Thursday. I know the perfect place for it. I'll fix up a picnic basket."

I knew the perfect place, too. All my nice summer reveries were dropping into place perfectly.

"I'll be ready," I said. "What time?"

"I'll meet you right here at eight o'clock."

I got out of the car and bent over and kissed her. "Don't be late."

"I won't be late this time. You can depend on it." She seemed to be hit by an idea. "Do you think you can get a bottle?"

"I'll get one," I said.

George was waiting impatiently. For some reason I think he actually expected I'd be bringing back the ring gear. I didn't even mention it.

"George," I said, "a couple of weeks ago you were talking about getting a bottle. Do you know where I can get one?"

"There's a fellow over in Curtis keeps a still, but you wouldn't want any of his stuff. One of the Finns gave me a snort of it one night and it burned the insides right out of me. They must have a state liquor store over in Newberry. What's all this stuff about whiskey all of a sudden?"

"I got a girl. I think I can get someplace with her."

Getting to Newberry was a real problem now. The Jacksons had gone home and I was effectively cut off from the only other good source of information I had about the movements of the various tourists. I had to walk over the trail to Jean's cove and go out on a point of land there and watch for Charlie to go out on the lake in his boat. When I saw him heading out with a fishing party about four in the afternoon, I ran for the camp and began knocking on cabin doors. There was a lady in Cabin Six who practically saved my life.

"Why, yes," she said. "John and I are going over to Newberry to the double feature. You can ride over with us. If you want to hang around until the movie is out we'll give you a ride home, too. How soon can you be ready to go?"

"I'm ready now."

"Good. We'll be leaving in about fifteen minutes. I want to get there before the A & P closes."

We made it to Newberry at quarter of six and I managed to slide in the door of the state liquor store just as the manager was getting ready to lock it. It was only nine months since Prohibition had been repealed and I didn't know one kind of whiskey from another, but I paid three dollars and a half for a quart of something.

When I walked out of the liquor store I had four hours to wait for my ride back home. I thought of going to the movie myself, but I'd just spent three dollars and a half and that was a lot of money for me. I kept telling myself that I only had six-fifty left and that was just enough to get George and me and the old car back across the Straits of Mackinaw. Although I'd been to Newberry several times now I'd never really seen the place so I decided to walk around and look it over. After wandering around for over an hour I came to a small park with benches in it. I sat there watching it get dark. There were quite a few people walking around, but none of them knew me, of course, or paid any attention to me. I began to feel lonely. When darkness finally descended, the people began to disappear and I was soon quite alone. I became conscious of the bottle I held in my hand and for some perverse reason, it seemed like a good time to try it. I unscrewed the cork and lifted it to my lips and took a little nip. It felt good going down and I was all warm inside so, when the warmness began to wear off, I took another nip. Still later, I took a third one. None of these nips were big ones and I most certainly hadn't taken enough to be drunk, but I wasn't used to drinking, especially straight whiskey. On top of that, I hadn't had anything to eat since breakfast. I definitely felt different. It was a kind of floating, far-off feeling. I suppose that I could have been transported in any one of three directions. I could have felt happy and gay— a sort of euphoria, or I might even have been inclined to lean back my head and take a nap. As it happened, however, about five minutes after I took that third nip, I felt a drop of rain. Soon the rain was coming down steadily. This was the first rain we'd had since we left Mackinaw City and it reminded me, somehow, of all the things that had gone wrong since we left home. I had to move, of course. I couldn't sit there on that park bench and let myself get soaked. I started walking along the street, keeping close to the store fronts, now and then ducking into a doorway. The farther I went, the more sorry I felt for myself. After two blocks I was quite morose. It was about then, I think, that I became conscious of those nickels I had taken out of Charlie Fuller's jackpot. I don't know why, now, but I had slipped them in my left-hand pocket away from my other money and as I stood there huddled over in the rain with my hands stuck deep in my pockets, the bottle under my arm, I began to play with them. A great light suddenly dawned on me. This was velvet. This was expendable. I didn't need it to get back across on the ferry. Across the street from me was a drugstore. I'm quite sure that what ensued would never have taken place if I hadn't had those three nips from the bottle. They were the catalyst that turned my unhappiness into indignation. I straightened up, took my hands out of my pockets, and walked resolutely across the street and into the drugstore. I went directly to the rear and pulled the nickels out of my pocket and put one in the pay phone. When the long distance operator answered I gave her our telephone number at home in Flint.

My brother Walter answered the call. The first words I said to him were "Where the hell is our ring gear?"

"What ring gear? What's a ring gear?"

I patiently explained what it was and then I asked him why he never read his mail.

"What mail?"

I was angry. While my brother Walter and I were fond of each other, we weren't exactly close. He had his own circle of friends and I had mine and a good deal of the time we went our separate ways. In any event, if I was going to write a letter at all, I wouldn't have written it to him. I would have written it to my father. All this escaped me entirely. As it slowly dawned on me that he wasn't aware of my predicament, indeed that he scarcely knew I'd been away from home for six weeks, I lit into him. I told him that I'd come all the way to the upper peninsula to check on Grandfather's property—after all, it was partly his—and that my car was broken down and I was broke. I thought it was about time someone down there paid attention. What started out to be an inquiry about the ring gear became a tirade. I can't remember all the things I told him, but I used up all those nickels I'd gotten from the slot machine.

My brother Walter must have been a little bewildered by what he heard. He had only been vaguely aware of where I was and what I was doing, but from the sound of my voice and the rush of words it was only natural that he would assume that I'd been overtaken by catastrophe. It was enough to make a person run out of the house and raise the populace. That's just about what he did. As for me, I walked out of the phone booth feeling as though I'd really accomplished something although I wasn't sure quite what it was. I think I rather expected someone might drop our ring gear by parachute the next morning.

I stood inside the drugstore until the movie let out and then I met the people from Charlie's camp. After they let me out of the car I walked through the rain down to the new tent we had set up and crawled in and went to sleep. When I woke up the next morning, things were absolutely awful. When we changed the location of the tent to get away from the worst of the skunk smell, we'd forgotten to dig ditches. We were on low ground anyway and now we were practically sleeping in the middle of a small lake. We were almost back to where we'd been that night in Mackinaw City and it was still raining hard. That wasn't the worst of it, however. George's first words contained bad news.

"You're not going to get any breakfast," he said.

"Why not?"

"Well, since we're not working for him any more, Charlie

has to carry all the ice himself. Last night when he was in the icehouse he found our food. He took it."

"He didn't take the Bisquick did he?"

"He took the whole works."

"My God!" I said. "It's a wonder we weren't murdered in our sleep."

"That's not what I'm worried about now. What I want to know is what are we going to eat? Did you get your bottle?"

"George, you're not thinking of drinking whiskey for breakfast, are you?"

"No, I'm not thinking of drinking whiskey for breakfast. I was thinking about that friend of mine over in Curtis. He likes a drink and if I gave him one it might be easier to get him to come over here and give us a tow."

"Are you sure you don't want to drink it yourself?"

"Oh, come on. You and your girl can't drink a whole quart. Pour me out some of it and I'll find a bottle to put it in and I'll take it with me when I go."

"How much?"

"I don't know. How about a cup?"

"A whole cup? George, that's a half pint. We don't want a drunken tow truck driver. I'll give you a half a cup."

"All right," he said. "A half cup." He looked around. "Let's get this thing ready to go." He pointed at the car.

We had plenty to do. In addition to putting the rear axle housing back on, we had to let the car down off the big pile of logs we had put under the rear end. I could see that the two front tires had gone flat during the long period we had been there. They hadn't blown out. The air had just slowly leaked out of them. I got out the hand pump while George went to work on the rear end. Fortunately for us, about ten minutes after we went to work, the rain stopped. A few minutes later the sun came out. It was a fairly hot sun for that time of the morning and it showed through a break in the trees directly on the spot we were working. The steam began to rise off our wet things. George eventually climbed out from under the car. He was dripping with perspiration.

"How about opening up that bottle now?" he asked me.

"That's not for you, George. That's for the tow truck driver. Remember?"

"If I never see you again after we get out of here it will be too soon," he said.

"Oh, all right, George, you can have it, only don't drink it all. That's all you're going to get." I went over and got one of our tin cups and poured him a half cup of whiskey and handed it to him. He took a swallow or two and then went over and set the cup down on our picnic table, then climbed under the car's rear end, and went back to work.

It couldn't have been more than ten minutes after he put that cup down when we had an interruption. Charlie's oldest daughter came walking down the hill. Although both George and I had been exposed to her during the weeks we worked and ate up at the house, neither one of us had had very much to do with her. She had just turned eleven a week before and she was most unattractive. Besides being big for her age, and ungainly, she was inclined to be brattish. Her main job was to keep that big common mowed, but during the weeks I worked she was forever trying to find ways to get me to do it for her. Sometimes she would attempt to use her wiles, of which she didn't have many. Other times she would try to bribe me. She most certainly wasn't above using threats. If, by some chance, a swear word slipped out when she was around, she would say, "I'm going to tell my daddy what you said unless you mow this part of the lawn for me." Now she stood there by the picnic table watching us work on the car.

"You're in trouble," she said finally.

I straightened up from my tire pumping and looked at her. "Go away," I said.

"You and your old Bisquick muffins. My daddy said he's coming down here and take it out of your hides." I didn't pay any attention to her. I went back to my tire pumping.

"My daddy said you are both no good. He said that you 'specially were no good."

I looked up to see who she was looking at. She was looking at me. She seemed to be peering at me as though she couldn't see me very well.

"Go away," I said again.

"He said anybody who let their hair grow long like you did was lazy and a lot of other things. He said you probably had lice in it. He said he was going to have to have the place fumigated just because you'd been in it."

I automatically put my hand up and felt my hair. It was pretty long. I hadn't had a haircut in about nine or ten weeks.

"Why don't you tie a ribbon on it?" She giggled.

George stuck his head out from under the car and looked at her. "If you don't get out of here and leave us alone, I'm going to paddle your big fat ass."

"Oh, what you just said. I'm going to tell my mother what you just said." She stumbled uncertainly toward the house.

"Good riddance," George said and stuck his head under the car again.

I was already back at work on the pump. "All that over three boxes of Bisquick. What do you suppose my hair has got to do with those muffins?"

"I don't know," George said. "Maybe you got some hair in the batter." He stuck his head out and looked at me. "That is pretty long, you know. Maybe you *had* better put a ribbon on it."

"You make any more remarks like that and I'll bend this pump around your head."

"No, I'm serious," he said. "You know those fellows in the movies—pirates and things. They always do their hair up in back and put a ribbon around it. They look good. Better than you. You're getting a little shaggy."

We continued to work. I finished the right front tire and

moved my pump around to the left front. George came out from under the car and began looking around.

"Where did I put that damned ring gear?" he said.

"Look under that pile of stuff over there on the end of the picnic table. What do you need the ring gear for? It's busted."

"I have to put it in there anyway. It sort of holds things together, even if there are only three teeth on it. It takes some of the strain off the rear axle." He walked over to the picnic table and rummaged around for a moment and picked up the ring gear. Then he reached out for the cup of whiskey.

"Hey!" he said, and then whirled to look up at the big house. "Why you little son of a bitch! You little bastard!"

"What's the matter?"

"That little bitch poured all my whiskey on the ground. I could kill her!"

"She could have drunk it," I said, and laughed. Then, all of a sudden I remembered the way she looked at me and stumbled as she walked off. "George!"

"What?"

"Maybe she *did* drink it!"

"Oh, no. If she'd drunk that she couldn't have walked from here to the tent over there." He pointed and I saw his hand freeze in mid-air. Slowly, as though in a trance, he stumbled toward the tent. "Oh, God!" he said.

I pushed the pump handle down and scrambled around the car and looked where he was pointing. There sprawled out on her back in the tent was Charlie's daughter.

"He'll kill us," I said.

"No, he won't. He'll make us marry her. You know, a shotgun wedding."

"Which one of us?"

"You, of course. It's your whiskey."

"Not me. He don't like me. My hair's too long."

"He'll probably burn it off with a blowtorch."

"George, all kidding aside, we're in trouble. You know Charlie. He's just mean enough to do something. If he ever found out that we gave his daughter a slug of whiskey he could have us arrested for all kinds of things. Like contributing to the delinquency of a minor, for instance. We could get fifteen years in jail."

"We didn't give it to her. She stole it."

"That won't make any difference. We've got to do something with her." I bent over and shook her. She didn't stir. "We've got to hide her so nobody will find her until she comes to. How long do you suppose she'll stay passed out like that?"

"I don't know. Two or three hours maybe. Maybe more if she was comfortable."

"Two or three hours isn't going to be enough."

"Enough for what?"

"To get this car out of here. I want to be just as far away from here as I can when she wakes up and starts blabbing."

"He'll follow us. He'll get a whole posse out after us."

"We'll just have to take a chance. Let's get her hid and then you beat it for Curtis and get that tow truck while I finish pumping up these tires."

"Where will we hide her?"

I looked all around. I thought of carrying her over in the thick bushes, but that was too much like getting rid of a corpse. My eyes finally lit on the big house.

"I think I know just the place," I said. "The hired man's room. Nobody ever goes down there since no one's staying down there."

"How are we going to get her there without anyone seeing us? There's thirty feet of open lawn between the woods here and the back door. Somebody's bound to see us."

I thought about it for a minute. "What we have to do is get everybody's attention somewhere else. Maybe if we yelled 'Fire' it would do the trick."

"It's not going to do any good to yell 'Fire' if you don't

have a fire. Everybody would just shrug their shoulders."

"Well, then, we'll set a fire."

"Good. Which cabin?"

"I don't want to set any cabin on fire. That's arson. What are you trying to do? Get us thrown in jail for life?"

"We got to set something on fire."

"We'll make a smudge over there on the other side of the common. You're good at making smudges. What do you need? Let's go."

"Grass," he said, "and sticks."

We began rushing around getting grass and sticks together and when we each had an armful, we circled up through the woods, keeping out of sight of the house. We picked a good spot about fifty yards from the house and George arranged everything. Then he started to light it. It wouldn't light. The matches were wet, the grass was wet, and the sticks were wet. Everything was wet from that all-night rain.

"Go and get some dry wood and matches," George hissed. "Quick."

"Where?"

"I don't care where."

I ran along the fringe of the common and came to Cabin Eleven. I peeked in the window and couldn't see anyone so I went to the kitchen door and banged on it. There was no answer so I turned the knob and let myself in. I was in the wrong cabin. Cabin Eleven was the newest one and Charlie had put an oilstove in it. I ran out the back door and down the hill toward Cabin Seven which I knew had a wood-burning stove. I knocked on the door and it swung open. A strange lady stood looking down at me.

"Well?" she said.

"Do you need any ice, lady? I'm supposed to fill up the iceboxes!"

"I'll look," she said.

I had to stand there and wait for her to come back.

"I'll take fifty pounds," she said, then looked around. "Where is it?"

"I have to go to the icehouse and get it."

I waved my hand at her and ran down the hill to Cabin Four. Once more I knocked on the door. There was no answer, so I let myself in. The wood box was full of dry wood. I grabbed up all there was and started out. As I did so, my eye caught sight of a box of wooden matches hanging in a container on the wall. I reached up and grabbed some. The whole container came off the wall and matches spilled all over the floor. I didn't bother to pick them up. I just turned and ran out the door and headed back for the upper part of the camp. George took the wood impatiently and rebuilt his fire. After what seemed like a long time, he lit a match to the newspaper at the bottom of the pile and the flames crept up the dry wood and caught. When it was burning good, George began dropping the grass on it. Great clouds of smoke began rising into the air. We didn't wait any longer. George headed back through the woods toward the camp and I ran out onto the common and stopped.

"Fire!" I shouted at the top of my voice. Then I ran for the big house and leaped up onto the porch and pushed open the front door. "Fire!" I shouted. "I think somebody dropped a cigarette in the woods." I could hear footsteps running across the kitchen. I didn't wait to see how many people were coming. I just ducked back out the door and ran down around the corner of the house to the back. I found George already trying to pull Charlie's daughter out of the tent.

"You'll have to help me," he shouted. "She's heavy."

I took her by the shoulders and he took her by the feet and we started for the big house. When we got to the edge of the open lawn, he stopped.

"Did you yell 'Fire'?"

I pointed. We could see a few people running across the common. He nodded and we stepped out into the open with our burden. We made it to the back door with a minimum of exposure and let ourselves in and put the girl down on the bed in the cubicle. I heaved a big sigh.

"Now get going," I said.

"Get going where?"

"To Curtis to get that tow truck."

"I can't."

"Why not?"

"I haven't finished putting it back together yet."

"Oh, goddamn it, George."

Something stirred beside us. I looked down. Charlie's daughter had one eye opened, cocked at us.

"You stop swearin'," she said. "I'm gonna tell my—" Her eye closed and she snored.

I shoved George out the back door and we ran for the tent. When we got there he swung himself down in back of the car.

"This will only take a minute," he said. "I'll just clap this axle housing on here and bolt it in place."

Actually, it didn't take him more than ten minutes. When he was done, he washed the grease off his hands.

"I'll take off now," he said. "When you get done pumping that tire up, take these logs out from under here. You'll have to use the jack to lift it a little so you can pull the logs out. You shouldn't have any trouble, but there's one more thing you ought to do. I've been thinking about it."

"What's that?"

"I think you ought to go back up there to the house and put a little glass of whiskey beside the bed."

"Why?"

"If she wakes up before we get out of here, she's going to start blabbing and Charlie will be right down here. We ought to have a story to tell."

"What kind of a story?"

"You can tell Charlie you don't know anything about any whiskey. She was just snooping around up there in the

218

hired man's room and she must have found it. We don't know anything about any whiskey."

"But supposing he starts snooping around this camp and finds the bottle?"

"Oh, I thought of that, too. Just give it to me and I'll take it with me."

"Go on! Get out of here!" I said. "You don't pull anything like that on me."

He shrugged and started up the hill toward the road. He'd gone only a few feet when he stopped.

"That's a good idea, anyway," he said. "If she wakes up and finds the whiskey she might drink it and go back to sleep again."

EIGHTEEN

It took George four hours to get to Curtis and get back with the tow truck. During that whole time I worked and fretted. I kept one eye peeled on the big house, fully expecting people to start issuing from it with shotguns and hatchets at any minute. Strangely enough, nothing happened. Either Charlie's daughter woke up and decided to keep her mouth shut, or else she was still asleep up there in the hired man's room. This was always a mystery to me and remains so to this day, for the keen noses of the Fullers would have been bound to pick up the scent of whiskey on the daughter's breath if she'd gone upstairs. Most certainly, she would have been missed and someone would have gone looking for her if she'd slept very long. The only thing that I've ever been able to figure out is that Mrs. Fuller must have taken the truck and gone into Manistique to do her shopping a day early.

In one way it was a good thing that George did take as long as he did. I had a lot to do. I finished pumping up the front tires about half an hour after George left and then began the task of getting the logs out from under the rear end. Jacking that car up was hard work. Everything we had was

221

stored in the big back seat, except for the tent and one or two pots and pans. It added so much weight that I found it almost impossible to lift with that antiquated jack of ours. I finally had to unload everything and pile it on the ground beside the car and that took a lot of time. There were three or four piles of things like iron skillets, suitcases, lanterns, and mackinaws. With them out of the car, however, I was able to lift the rear axle enough to yank the pile of logs out of there and let the wheels down onto the ground. That brought on more hard work. The back tires had also lost all their air and I had to go to work with the hand pump again. All this was on an empty stomach.

That part of it was relieved, fortunately. I had just finished inflating the last of the rear tires and was sitting on the running board, all hot and sweaty, to rest, when I heard a shout from up on the road. There was George climbing down out of the cab of a dilapidated old pickup truck. I could see him giving the driver instructions, and then the truck began backing down the hill between the trees as George stood in front and helped with the guiding. When the vehicle came to rest a few feet in front of our car, the driver began to crawl out of his seat and George opened the door on the other side and took out a paper bag. He brought it over and handed it to me.

"Give Olie a dollar," he said, "and don't ask any questions or do any griping."

I reached in my pocket and pulled out a dollar bill and handed it to the driver, then looked in the bag. There were three hamburgers and a small bottle of milk in it. I was never so glad to see anything in my life.

"Go ahead and eat it," George said. "I had mine over at Curtis."

I stood there munching on the hamburgers and drinking the milk while George and Olie got an old rope out of the back of the truck. They tied one end of it around the front axle of our car and the other end to the back of the truck.

"All right," George said. "Now get that bottle of whiskey out and let's all have a slug and then we'll get going."

I didn't feel like protesting. I went over to the tent and pulled the bottle out from between the blankets and passed it to Olie. He took a good pull at it and passed it to George. When George handed it to me I was about to take my own drink, but when I looked at it I saw that there was only a little over half of it left. That wasn't much more than enough to get Jean MacKenzie started. I put the cork back in the bottle.

"All right, Olie," George said. "Let's go!"

"Wait a minute!" I said, and waved my arm around the campsite. "We're not going to leave all this good camping equipment here for Charlie."

"We haven't time to load it," George said. "Olie can only have this truck for an hour. We can come back later and pick it up. Maybe MacKenzie will lend us a boat and we can row over and get it."

I looked at Olie and I could see he was anxious to get moving. I didn't feel like arguing anyway. I just crawled up in the front seat beside George. The truck inched ahead and the tow rope pulled taut. Silently and triumphantly we began to glide up out of the woods. When we reached the road and turned into it, I looked at my watch. It was just twenty minutes after six. I think the date was August 30, 1934. Our troubles were over—almost.

We moved slowly through the thick woods and down the long hill from Charlie's camp, eventually reaching that big rock where I had sat and stewed so many times. Olie swung his truck to the left and we rolled out onto the new road that the CCC had built. It seems strange to me, now, but after all those weeks I was traveling that road for the very first time. If I had ever wondered about it—why it had taken so many years before anyone tried to build it—my eyes were about to be opened. The area across which we were now traveling was a swamp. It was really an arm of Big Manistique Lake—a long arm that stretched a mile or more inland from the western shore. It was a good two miles wide, perhaps more. There were large expanses of dark, murky water with little hummocks sticking up out of it. In actuality the road was nothing but a long causeway that stretched from island to island. It had been built by hauling in thousands of cubic yards of dirt. A good part of this dirt had promptly sunk out of sight as soon as it was dumped, for the swamp seemed almost bottomless and it became evident quite early that there were wide areas of quicksand. In order to give some base to the road the CCC boys had cleared stumps and other logging debris and had dug up rocks from all over that part of the upper peninsula and had dumped it in the swamp along with the dirt. When the causeway was finished it was topped off with a corduroy. A corduroy was a standard device used in logging days in swampy areas. Logs are laid crossways, much like railroad ties, and dirt is poured over them.

The building of that road across the swamp was truly a remarkable engineering feat for Manistique swamp turned out to be a formidable obstacle. The pity of it was that it had already become apparent that the job was not likely to be permanent. On that evening that we turned into the road, it was not yet six months old and it had already begun to sink out of sight. In some places it had sunk so far that the water lapped within six inches of the wheel tracks. It was a single lane road for most of its traverse of the swamp and the only places where cars could pass each other were at the points where the trail crossed one or another of those little islands. To make matters worse, as the road slowly sank into the morass the dirt part of it sank faster than the transverse logs of the corduroy so that a car bumped along from log to log. It was, indeed, a lot like driving along railroad ties.

Up until the moment we rolled out onto that corduroy, we moved along smoothly, but when we began to bump along over those logs, it was apparent we were going to have trouble. We'd gone scarcely a quarter of a mile when the right rear tire, unable to stand the pounding, blew out with a large bang. The truck stopped and Olie came back to take a look, but George shook his head.

"The goddamned tire is shot, anyway," he said. "We're going to have to buy new ones when we get it over to Mac-Kenzie's. The hell with changing it. We'll just run it on in the way it is."

We bumped along for another two hundred yards and the left front let go with a whistling noise. This was the one tire, incidentally, that hadn't given us any trouble since we started out. Olie stopped again, but George waved to him to go ahead and grimly fought the steering wheel as we moved out again. We made another half mile and then, suddenly, the back began to sway wildly from side to side. A moment passed and the whole rear end of the car seemed to sag out from underneath us. We dragged along a few feet and then the tow rope broke. George and I slowly got out of the car and Olie came walking back. We were in one of those narrow spots in the road where the water had risen to a point less than a foot from the running board of the car. I had to tightrope in order to keep from stepping in the swamp.

Our damage was major. One might almost call it mortal. After we had carried Charlie's daughter up to the big house, George had been in such a hurry to get out of the camp that he'd just clapped the axle housing on without putting the ring gear back in place. There had been nothing to help take up the strain on the rear axle and the jolting of the corduroy had snapped it. The right rear wheel had come off. The left rear wheel was leaning crazily against the fender.

"We've got to jack it up and put those wheels back on and tie that axle together some way so that it will get us over to MacKenzie's," George said.

225

"Gosh, George," Olie said. "That's going to take a long time and I can't hang around here until you fix it. What you really need now is a real tow truck, one with a crane that can lift that back end up in the air."

"You got any of those over in Curtis?"

"Shucks, no. There's probably one in Manistique. Maybe in Newberry. You'd have to call and find out."

"How much do you figure they'd charge to come and get this thing?"

"Ten dollars. I don't know."

"That's almost as much as the car is worth." George shook his head. "I guess we'll just have to fix it ourselves. I'll tell you what you do, Olie. You go on back home. When we get it ready to move, I'll call you."

Olie shrugged, uncertainly. "I don't like to leave you guys out here like this, but I don't see what else I can do."

"Go ahead, Olie."

We watched him walk back up to his truck and climb in. We stood there looking after him until he was lost to our sight.

"Well, George, what do we do?"

He explained it to me. The whole axle wasn't lying on the ground. First we had to jack up the part that was already in the air, put some logs under it, then move the jack along and jack up more and put logs under that part. Eventually, when we got it all off the ground we would have to jack it all up higher and put more logs under it until we got it up to the point where we could put the wheels on easily. The rear axle housing would have to come off and there were a few other odds and ends that had to be done. I didn't understand all of it, but just from the length of time it took him to explain it, I figured we'd be there for two days.

"I guess the first thing we'd better do is to find some logs to put under there when we get it jacked up," he said.

For once we were lucky. About a hundred yards back along the road, on one of those little islands, the CCC

226

boys had stacked an enormous pile of logs to use in the corduroy. We carried about twenty of them to the car and got out the jack and went to work. We had most of the axle off the ground and were putting our last logs under it when a car came around the corner behind us from Germfask. It was beginning to get dark and the driver had turned his lights on. He pulled up behind us and waited for a moment or two, then blew his horn, a long insistent blast. George turned around and looked. There were a man and a woman in the car. The horn blew again. George straightened up and walked slowly back and addressed the driver.

"What are you blowing your horn for?" he asked.

"I want to get by," the man said in a high, shrill voice. "I want you to move your car."

"How?" George said.

"I don't care how. Just get it out of the way."

"What's the matter with your eyesight?" George said. "You can see the car is broken down. There's no way I can move it. If you're in a real hurry, you'd better go back and down through Blaney."

"Are you crazy, man? That's more than thirty miles out of my way."

George shrugged. "Suit yourself. We're doing the best we can here. Just don't blow that horn any more."

We went back to work and soon had the last of our logs firmly in place.

"I guess we'd better go back and get some more logs before we do anything else," George said.

In order to get to the pile of logs on the island we had to walk by the car that was still sitting there. We had taken about ten steps past it when there was another long, insistent blast on the horn. George turned around and went back to the car.

"I thought I told you not to blow that horn any more."

"But you were just walking off and leaving that car there in the middle of the road."

George nodded. Without saying a word he went on up to our car and bent over and picked up the metal jack handle. He brought it back and held it up for the driver to see.

"We were just going back to get some more logs. If you were in a real hurry and if you had any sense of decency about you, you'd get out of there and help us carry some logs, but all you want to do is sit there like an idiot and blow your horn. Well, I'll tell you something, mister. You blow that horn just once more and I'll put this jack handle right through your windshield." He turned and went back and stuck the handle back in the jack and then rejoined me. We carried about ten more logs back and put two of them in place and then George reached for the jack.

"That's funny," he said. "Where's the handle to this thing?"

We crawled around on our hands and knees. It was no place to be found.

"Let's sit down and have a cigarette," he said. We lit up and George leaned back against one of the fenders, looking up at the dark sky, puffing away as though he was relaxed for the night. When he finished the first cigarette he lit up a second one. He was about halfway through that one when a second set of headlights came around the corner from Germfask and pulled up behind the first car. A big burly man got out of the new car and walked forward.

"Having trouble, boys?" he said, and looked over our car. When he'd done, he turned back to us. "Don't you think it would be a good idea to get to work fixing it instead of just sitting there on your ass?"

"We were fixing it," George said, "but that son of a bitch back there stole our jack handle. Now we can't do anything."

The man scratched his head. "Why would he want to do a thing like that?"

"I don't know. You'll have to ask him."

The big man strolled calmly back to the first car and looked down at the driver.

"Those boys tell me you took their jack handle. Did you?"

A woman's voice spoke up. "That man up there threatened to break our windshield with it."

"Will you shut up, Bunny?" the driver said, and then evidently addressed himself to the big man. "We don't know anything about any jack handle."

The big man shook his head and came back to us. "What's this about threatening to break their windshield?"

"Look," George said, "we were working away here, trying to get this thing fixed. This fellow, there, came up behind us and started blowing his horn. I told him we were doing the best we could and to stop blowing his horn. He kept right on blowing it. I stood it as long as I could and then I told him to stop blowing it or I'd throw the jack handle through his damned windshield."

"I don't know but what I'd have done the same thing, boys. I might even have thrown the jack handle." He turned and walked back along the road and stopped at the other car. "Just what did you do with that jack handle?" he said.

"He threatened us with it," the woman whined.

"I don't care what he did with it. What I want to know is what *you* did with it."

"Out there," the woman shrieked. "He threw it out there." She pointed at the swamp.

"I see," the big man said. "Now wasn't that a fine thing to do? How did you expect those boys to get their car fixed?"

"But he was going to break our windshield," the woman whined.

"I don't like people who throw jack handles in swamps," the big man said. "It's a pretty lousy trick."

"All right," the driver said, his voice shrill and nasty, "you don't like us. We'll accept that. The thing is, I want to get where I'm going. Would you please be kind enough to back your car up out of the way? We'll go around by way of Blaney."

"Tomorrow morning maybe I'll back it out of the way. Or maybe tomorrow night. Who knows?" The big man shrugged. "I'm tired and I think I'll go to sleep. Who knows when I'll wake up?" He started to walk back to his car, but the other driver stuck his head out of his.

"You can't do that," he yelled. "You've got us blocked in here. We can't get out."

"It's true you're not going to back out of here," the big man said. "Not until hell freezes over, you're not. Of course, if those boys got their jack handle back and got their car fixed, you might get out that way." He walked back and got in his car and slammed the door. A moment later his headlights went out. I assumed he had laid his head back and gone to sleep.

George and I just sat there, smoking our cigarettes and enjoying the summer night. We could hear the man and the woman arguing. About twenty minutes after the big man got back in his car, the door of the first car opened and the driver got out. It was now completely dark, but a big, round full moon was rising in the east and it was bathing the whole scene in a soft light. We watched while the driver sat down on his running board and took off his shoes and sox and rolled up his pants. When he was ready, he stepped over to the edge of the road and timidly stuck his foot down into the cold water, drew it back and shook it, then stuck it in again. Then he put his other foot in. He was up to his knees in that first step. When he took his second step he went right down out of sight. He came to the surface, let out a yell, and began to sink again. George and I jumped to our feet and picked up a log and ran toward him. We thrust the log out into the water and the man grabbed hold of it and hung on for dear life. The big man came running up from his car and gave us a hand in pulling the log back in. We finally got the driver back up on the road. He stood there dripping muddy water from head to foot.

"Now look what you made me do," he yelled.

"Go over and stand in front of your car and have your wife blow the horn," the big man said. "Maybe the wind from it will dry you out." He turned to us and shook his head. "Boys, I don't think you're going to get your jack handle back. We'd better figure out something else."

"Do you have a jack in your car we can use?" George asked.

"I don't know. I'll look."

He was still rummaging around in the trunk of his car when a set of headlights swung into the road ahead of us, coming from Curtis. At almost the same time, two other cars swung the corner from Germfask and pulled up behind the two cars that were already there. The drivers all got out and came to look the situation over. There were also three extra fishermen in one of the cars so that we had quite a crowd. George explained what we were trying to do. Everyone chipped right in to help us. While some of the men carried logs, others got the car jacked up. George was just beginning to put the wheels into place when those round logs started to roll and the next thing we knew the whole back end was down on the ground again. There was some very picturesque language being thrown around there, I can tell you. It was while we were still standing there swearing that another car pulled up from Curtis. A door slammed and the next thing I knew, Alec MacKenzie walked into the light. He walked all around the car looking at it with his hand on his chin.

"Aye, it's a mess, lads," he said. "I do not think ye'll get it repaired, either. Even if ye get the wheels on this time, it will only roll about a hundred or two hundred yards down the road before they come off again. That's if ye're lucky." He shook his head. "Who owns this car?" I stepped forward and he looked at me. "Don't I know ye from some place, lad?"

I gave him my name.

"Ah, I thought ye'd flown the coop. Where've ye been, lad? I've been lookin' for ye."

"You should have asked your granddaughter. She knew all the time."

"Did she now? I never thought of that. I even wrote your father a letter the other day." He looked at the car and shook his head again. "This is bad, laddie. I'm expectin' a lot of people at my camp for the weekend and as long as this thing is blocking the road, none of them can get there. What's this car worth to ye, lad?"

"I paid twenty dollars for it," I said.

"That was when it was in running condition, which it is not now. I'll give ye five dollars for it just as it is now, just as it stands."

I looked at George. I don't know what I expected him to do or say. To my surprise, he nodded.

"Sold," I said.

Alec MacKenzie pulled out his pocketbook and counted our four one-dollar bills and two fifty-cent pieces and handed them to me. Then he turned and waved at all the other people.

"Everybody lend a hand here," he said. He directed them all to line up along one side of the car and take hold of something. "All right, lads, when I say the word, everybody heave-ho. One—two—three and in she goes!"

The car slowly tilted on its side and then toppled, landing in the water with a big splash. I watched it as it slowly sank from sight, stern first. It was a little like watching the sinking of the *Titanic*. It hadn't even settled yet when Alec MacKenzie had the men clearing the logs off the road. Before he went back and got in his car, he came over to me.

"Ye go on over to my camp, lads. Tell the manager to give ye a bed. I'll see ye in the morning." He turned and started telling each of the car drivers how to back up or go ahead so that the traffic jam would be broken. Within five minutes George and I were standing there in the moonlight, all alone. All we could see of our old car was the radiator and the two front tires sticking up out of the water. Strangely enough, my last sight of it was quite fitting. There was that same old hole on the right front tire as big as a half dollar. It was the only tire we had which had not blown out.

"Well," George said, "let's get on over to MacKenzie's camp."

"Not tonight," I said. "I don't like the idea of leaving all that equipment of ours over there in Charlie's place. He could sell it before morning. We'll go over to MacKenzie's tomorrow morning and borrow that boat."

We strolled back to Charlie Fuller's in a very leisurely fashion. We sat there in the moonlight at our picnic table until the lights were all out up in the big house and then we built our fires. It was midnight when we finally crawled in our tent and went to sleep.

We slept three hours and a half. I was awakened by the sound of loud voices outside our tent. Someone had thrown a lot of wood on our fire and it was burning brightly. I looked at George. His eyes were wide open.

"Charlie must have got his posse together," he whispered. "Is there any way we can sneak out of here?"

I didn't have a chance to answer. Someone suddenly pulled the pegs that held our main guy ropes and the tent collapsed in my face. I flailed around and fought to find an opening, finally sticking my head out from under the edge. A pail of water caught me full in the face and someone howled with glee as I sputtered. A moment later I heard George yell as he got his pail of water over the head. I wiped the water out of my eyes and looked around. The first person that came into focus was my brother Walter. Across the tent from him stood Lou Norris, an old friend of George's and mine from high-school days. Even as I watched, they turned and started picking up our equipment to throw it in the back of Lou's roadster.

"What the hell do you guys think you are doing?" I shouted.

"Get out of that tent and start helping a little," my brother said. "We want to catch the eight o'clock ferry at St. Ignace."

I climbed to my feet and stumbled around, trying to pick things up. Suddenly I straightened up.

"Hey!" I said. "We can't go home today. I've got a date tonight."

"I've got a date tonight, too," Lou said. "Mine's in Flint. Where is yours?"

"Right here. I'm supposed to go swimming with a girl. I've been working on it all summer."

"I don't care if you're going swimming bare-assed with her. We're going home."

"That's just what I was planning on doing," I said. "How did you know?"

He didn't say anything. I picked up some equipment and put it in the car, all the time thinking about Jean. I finally had an idea.

"I just remembered. I'm supposed to talk to Alec MacKenzie in the morning."

"Alec who?"

"Alec MacKenzie. He wants to buy that property."

"Oh, him," said my brother. "Don't worry about him. The old man had a letter from him yesterday. He offered a hundred dollars for it."

"A hundred bucks?" I stood there thinking about it.

"Look!" my brother said. "Will you get busy? I took two days off from my job to come up here and rescue you. Do you know what this weekend is?"

"No."

"It's Labor Day. Everybody and his brother will be heading for home. By this afternoon there'll be a line ten miles long waiting for that ferry. We wouldn't get home until next Wednesday."

I looked at George for help.

"Don't look at me," he said. "I never want to see the upper peninsula again as long as I live." He bent over and began folding the tent.

We reached Germfask and made the turn for Blaney at five o'clock. From my place in the rumble seat where I'd been stuffed in with the equipment, I looked over at MacKenzie's house. The last thing I saw as we went over the hill was Jean MacKenzie coming down the front steps in her one-piece bathing suit, a white towel around her neck.

Lou Norris drove like a madman and we reached St. Ignace just in time to make the eight o'clock ferry. The same captain was up on the bridge as we drove aboard and the ramp swung up behind us, but he didn't recognize us. We reached Grayling around two in the afternoon and Lou turned around to look at me.

"Hey! George says you got a bottle. How about giving us all a snort?"

I thought about it. "I can't," I said. "The bottle's at the bottom of Manistique swamp."

George turned around and looked at me. "What do you mean?" he asked.

"I just remembered. When we towed that car out of the camp, I had it in my hand. I didn't want Charlie coming down there and throwing it all on the ground so I took it along. It's still sitting there on the front seat of the car."

"It'll float out into the lake and Charlie will get it anyway," George said.

"No, it won't. Some morning Jean will dive in the water and there it will be. It's hers anyway."

235

EPILOGUE

A week after I got home, my father called me and asked me to come over to his office. When I walked in, I found Alec MacKenzie sitting there. He didn't seem very happy.

"Mr. MacKenzie came all the way down here to see us."

"I didn't hear from ye," Alec MacKenzie said, "and the lad, here, left without seein' me. I want to buy that property, if it's not been sold."

"It hasn't been sold," I said.

"Are ye sure, lad? Ye've not been dickering with Charlie Fuller?"

"What makes you think I'd be dickering with Charlie Fuller?"

"I learned from my granddaughter that ye've been staying at his camp all summer. If ye've not made a deal with him, I'm prepared to make ye an offer, right now. I've got the cash in my pocket."

"What's your offer?"

He looked at me a long time. "Five hundred dollars," he said. "Whatever offer Charlie made you, I don't think he'll meet that."

"I'm certain of it," I said. "You've got a deal."

I'm afraid Charlie had the last word, however. Alec Mac-Kenzie never did get around to developing that property. As far as I know it still sits there, covered with poison ivy. Twenty years later, in 1954, George took his sons fishing in the upper peninsula. In the course of the trip he couldn't resist taking the boys around to show them Charlie's camp. Charlie was still there, dogtrotting from chore to chore at the age of seventy. George walked out past the barn to the pasture where we used to drive the cows and he had to pass the sawmill. He thought he heard a familiar sound and looked in. There, driving the saws, was the motor from that old 1916 Buick. Charlie had gone over to the swamp one night after we left and had fished the old car out. He couldn't use the tires, but he did use the motor.

George didn't give me any report on the cove. I assumed that Jean was no longer there.